THE OC

'Twas the Night Before Chrismukkah

by A. Van Syckle

Based on the television series created
by Josh Schwartz

SCHOLASTIC INC.
New York   Toronto   London   Auckland   Sydney
Mexico City   New Delhi   Hong Kong   Buenos Aires

No part of this work may be reproduced in whole or in part, stored in a retrieval system, or transmitted in any form or by any means, electronic, mechanical, photocopying, recording, or otherwise, without written permission of the publisher. For more information regarding permission, write to Scholastic Inc., Attention: Permissions Department, 557 Broadway, New York, NY 10012.

ISBN 0-439-74571-3

Published by Scholastic Inc.

SCHOLASTIC and associated logos are trademarks and/or registered trademarks of Scholastic Inc.

12 11 10 9 8 7 6 5 4 3 2 1   5 6 7 8 9/0

Printed in the U.S.A.
First printing, December 2005

Ryan Atwood looked across the pool into the vast horizon of lush green manicured lawns that rolled through the hills of Newport Beach like the waves below. He took a deep breath and bit the inside of his lip until he had control over his tears. He knew he should be happy standing with a closet full of clothes, a family, and the brother he had found in Seth, but it was hard to forget the past. Even now it was harder than he had imagined.

Ryan had spent his life wondering why Santa never came to his house. The Christmas tree was usually a haphazard mess of homemade ornaments created out of tinfoil, stale popcorn strung on thread, and a cardboard star he knew his mother had stolen from a beer advertisement at the convenience store. His house had never been a happy one at Christmas. The pressure surrounding the holidays seemed to make his mother do everything with greater intensity. She smoked more, drank more, and skipped work more.

Ryan and his brother had found solace in their neighbors. Theresa and her family had been a source of kindness. They didn't have money but they took time to make sure there was laughter in the house and it was filled with smells of cloves, oranges, and pine. Theresa's mother loved Christmas because she could break out the pine-scented air spray. Everyone had fake trees in Chino. It was too expensive to buy a real tree year after year, and Theresa's mother sprayed pine on every sprig of the imitation branches as they set it up.

Ryan knew that in his neighborhood right now there were kids on the streets looking for promises from Santa. Promises that would lead to empty rooms, no presents, and even worse times when there were no parents to hold them with loving arms. Those were things a kid never forgot — not even as an adult.

Don't look back, Ryan thought.

"It will never be like that again," he whispered to himself.

But Ryan knew that life was uncertain and Trey, his brother, had let him down often enough to teach him that people never change. No matter how hard they tried. It was even harder to escape the ghetto's code of honor if it was in your blood. His mother never changed. One hundred new starts and she would always wind up drinking again. Ryan had wished Trey was smarter but he knew temptation was always the enemy.

Temptation ran highest at Christmastime. Who couldn't help but notice all the things you didn't have when the store windows were filled with beautiful sweaters, watches, sunglasses, cool new iPods, digital cameras, video phones, and portable PlayStations? Now that he moved among the rich, slipping between them at parties and functions, he had developed enough chameleon skin to fit in, except when it came to his pockets. Ryan always felt like an imposter. His clothes — his outward appearance — were marked by purchases and indulgences from hip stores like Fred Segal, reflecting Sandy's generosity and Kirsten's good taste, but his pockets still had holes.

It wasn't that Kirsten and Sandy didn't give him an allowance — they were more than generous and he knew if he asked for anything they would help; it was that he hated asking. Asking for help was like defeat. It meant he wasn't able to stand on his own anymore. He knew he had softened. Christmas was a time when emotions ran high and he would be damned if after all this time being hard he would break down and cry.

"Stop it," he said out loud to himself and ran to the bathroom to wash his face with cold water.

"No fair, dude, I haven't even told you what I am brewing for the new seasonal festivities. Give me a chance to dance, man," Seth whined and threw himself dramatically on the couch, pretending to punch the pillows like a kid having a tantrum. "Waaaa, no one wants to play with me this year. Waaa, I want to make yarmulke gingerbread cookies!"

Ryan had been so deep in thought he hadn't even seen Seth walk across the patio toward him in the pool house. Seth looked up from the couch and was about to start ranting about how expensive the gifts were on Summer's "I've been good" list but when he looked at Ryan he stopped. It couldn't be. Ryan looked like he had puffy eyes and the sallow face he got when things weren't going well. Seth thought, for just a moment, that Ryan had been crying. He shook his head, unable to digest the thought.

"Hey. Before exams start I want to talk about our theme for Chrismukkah," he said.

"No." Ryan smiled.

He really believed Seth was his brother. His feelings for Trey were all mixed up. He loved Trey out of duty but not always as a person. He loved Seth because he was just Seth. Seth was silly, misunderstood, deep, smart, and longing for acceptance and love from people who didn't matter. Ryan wanted to talk but didn't know how. Why was it so easy for Seth? Seth never stopped talking. He could go on and on about his emotions or nothing at all and never once felt ashamed of sharing his volcanic spewing of feelings and thoughts. Ryan rubbed his eye.

"Is there something on your mind, Ryan?" asked Seth.

"No," he shot back, sucking in his breath and now biting his tongue by accident.

"Okay." Seth knew he should tread lightly. "So, you want to hear my great idea for this year's blowout Chrismukkah? I think we should do a whole theme park around the pool. We could make a manger and then put the menorah on the diving board."

"The what?"

"The menorah. I explained this once already. That is what Jewish people do to celebrate Hanukkah. It was all about how they expected only one day of light from some oil and then every day the oil lasted another day and finally after eight days it went out."

"So the point is?" Ryan asked, deciding to let Seth lead the conversation.

"It's kind of like a candelabra with added value."

"And the point then is?"

"Oh — to remember that miracles happen and that suffering is never very far away."

"Well, that's for sure." Ryan felt tired out by Seth suddenly. He knew it was just a small jealousy that Seth never had to look in the windows of stores and ask for things he'd never get.

"Why the sour face?"

"Why the need to push?"

"Okay, let's drop it. Now back to my idea about a funny, very California-like Chrismukkah water park. I mean, it's perfect. There is the whole symbolism of water being a purifying factor in religion."

"Seth — that is a pool. Not a baptismal font."

"Yes, but this is Chrismukkah and you are not showing vision, imagination, or enthusiasm."

Ryan knew he should walk away but Seth was just pushing too hard.

"Maybe not all of us love this time of year."

"What's not to love? It's amazing. The sun is out; people put fake snow all over their lawns and string up enough lights that it looks like Vegas! It's a total blast with parents indulging the ones they love with insanely expensive gifts, which of course I feel I wholeheartedly deserve after living through some serious fiascos, and best of all they spend so much time at Christmas cocktail parties that they are wasted for three weeks." As soon as the words slipped out of Seth's mouth he knew what was wrong.

He looked apologetically at Ryan but Ryan was staring at the floor with his hands in such tight fists they were turning white. Seth took a deep breath and realized the more he knew about Ryan, there were still so many times he was wrong. He wished Ryan would go to therapy. It was normal for everyone he knew to go to therapy. Seth was so good at communicating his feelings that his own therapist had told him he didn't need to come back and he was a great, adjusted, loving, wonderful boy. At the time he had wondered, *If I am so great, why does everyone call me Wonder Geek, Chicken Legs, and Skate Spud?* It had been Ryan who had given Seth the confidence to overcome the very things his therapist could never help him do: talk to women. Not just talk to women but love them and be loved by them. Ryan had helped Seth to stop being a boy and look forward to being a man, but he could never tell him without breaking all the rules of being a guy.

Ryan looked Seth in the eye.

"I know what I said, Ryan. I'm sorry. I'm really sorry."

Ryan felt like he was going to break. Maybe now after these few years living in comfort he could finally be safe enough to deal with his past.

Ryan leaned forward on his chair and opened his mouth but nothing came out.

Seth leaned forward on the sofa and started to wave Ryan on as if they were playing charades.

Ryan inhaled and then sat back in his chair. He looked at the ceiling. It seemed easier this way.

"You just never forget, man," he said, his voice cracking.

Ryan thought about the year he turned six and his mother was going to spend Christmas in jail for her second drunk driving offense. No one had been able to help them: not the lawyers, not the cops, not even Santa Claus. It was a Christmas that had stained the holiday forever. A prison family room was a horrible place no matter what time of year it was, and on Christmas the odor of fake cheer, burned cookies, and desperation was as bad as the gaudy tinsel and synthetic Santa hats they gave all the children.

Seth felt stupid because he wanted to ask, "Forget what?" but instead he kept his mouth shut and nodded gently. He was acting like Allan Jones, the award-winning, book-writing, scholarly, well-rewarded psychologist; in short, Seth was trying to get Ryan to talk by being quiet. Something he founder harder to do than Ryan understood.

Marissa Cooper waited at the Bliss Spa for Summer. She had already been there for fifteen minutes and the woman behind the desk had grown agitated.

"Are you sure she's coming?" asked the receptionist.

Marissa had dialed Summer's cell phone three times without luck.

If it had been anyone else but Summer, Marissa would have worried, but Summer had something that always kept her steady. Summer had the ability to shove her way to the front of the line at any restaurant, movie theater, or boutique and feel justified about doing it. Her confidence was something Marissa envied. Although Marissa knew she was popular and many people saw her as lucky for all of her beautiful clothes, her small figure, and the ability to manage events, she often felt ashamed, depressed, even embarrassed. Her mother's

constant dramas had always overshad-
owed her own. She felt lost in the shuffle
between being a pretty play toy for her
mother to dress and show off and being
the bad girl her mother was ashamed of
and wanted to put away in an institution.
As good as it looked from the outside,
Marissa Cooper was usually sad and afraid
of how her life would turn out. She also
knew that Summer had one thing she
had lost, not for good, but by distance:
Jimmy, her father. Summer's dad always
called to say she was beautiful and perfect
and that he loved her even when he didn't
see her. Jimmy's new job sailing often took
him out of cell phone reach and it seemed
that when Marissa needed him most she
always got his voice mail.

Summer blew through the door, fraz-
zled. It was rare for Marissa to see Summer
so agitated.

The woman behind the desk gave her a cold stare.

"I imagine you are Summer Roberts?"

"No need to *imagine*. I am the real thing."

"Miss Roberts, here at Bliss we make every effort to keep our schedules operating at maximum efficiency for our busy customers."

"As if? These are all women of the OC. They don't have anywhere else to go but Miu Miu."

"Summer!" Marissa giggled. Again Marissa was impressed by Summer's frank attitude and inability to be manipulated by adults. She just wasn't scared of people the way Marissa was.

"Miss Roberts, everyone is busy and regardless of where they are going you need to be here fifteen minutes before your treatment begins, not fifteen minutes after."

Summer did not hide the exaggerated rolling of her eyes and flopped herself down next to Marissa.

"She must be from the East Coast."

"I called you three times. What's up?" asked Marissa.

"My father is going away. There is some major crisis with a princess and she needs to have her face fixed before the holidays."

"Wow, that is so cool. They called your dad. I'd be so proud. Your dad gets the plastic surgeon's award like every year."

"Yeah, yeah — he's the golden boob man."

"Hey, why are you so upset?"

"Well, I know the princess of some country near Switzerland was thrown from her horse and they want my dad to put her royal nose back together but he is going to be away right up until Christmas!"

"Oh. So you'll be alone?"

"Basically. My stepmonster will be

dipping into the prescriptions and watching colorized versions of movies she says she is way too young for but totally remembers."

"That sounds like fun."

"Fun? *Fun*? Sitting around with my teary bleary-eyed stepmonster eating fat-free popcorn while she cries over a movie where it's all a dream and some guy has a wonderful life even though it sucks?"

"Summer, I think you are taking this a little hard. Your dad is the best in his field. I'd be proud. Besides, you'll have me."

"Why? I thought you were going to visit your dad."

"No, my dad wants to take care of some things here and he says he misses Sandy and, ya know, Kirsten, and he wants to come back for Christmas."

Summer jumped up and threw her arms around Marissa. She was jumping up and down so fast, squealing with delight, that it almost choked Marissa. But there was something Marissa felt that she hadn't in a long time: unconditional love. Her best friend really loved her. They were BFF: *Best Friends Forever*, the kind who would be together no matter what happened, and never fall for the same guy, amen! It was a pretty sure deal that no one could come between them. Marissa wrapped her arms around Summer and held her tightly, absorbing how nice it felt to get a hug from someone who likes you just as you are, no matter what.

Summer spoke softly, "Uh, Coop. You're pushing this. I mean, it's starting to feel like a funny girl hug — not like a girly hug but like a strange thing you've done but I am so not into and I love you so much and whatever is cool but you're kind of touching my lower back."

Marissa started to laugh so hard. She wanted to tell Summer right then, right there, that was the best gift she had ever gotten for Christmas, a real hug with no fake air kissing to save your lip gloss. But from the look on Summer's face and the two technicians waiting to give them their pedicures, she didn't think now was the time.

She cocked her head to the large rainbow of new hot holiday colors and said, "Are you doing traditional red or high volume?"

Summer looked relieved and snapped three shades of red from the display. "I think I am going Mistletoe Berry." She looked panicked again.

Marissa slugged her on the arm. "Don't worry, Summer, even if I liked you in a funny way I would never stoop to kissing your toes!"

"Oh, do you think Seth would?" she asked.

"I think Seth already does."

2

Seth was in his element. He prowled around the deep sunken living room like a mad scientist excited to propose his plan. Summer rolled her eyes. It reached a point since the second comic book fiasco that she was wary of anything Seth got too excited about. She had lost faith in his motives and his ability to tell the whole truth. She had begun to feel there were times she had given Seth all the tools to be a man and now he liked to take them out for use without telling her. The game was getting old and she would find herself thinking back to Zach's sincerity or brilliance. . . . or maybe she just liked the idea of being with someone who didn't only think about himself. It would be nice if Seth went back to obsessing about her.

Marissa had just a little schnapps before leaving the house. The idea that she had to sit down in one room with Ryan and her mother was more than she could bear. Since the entire crew would be there, she knew she needed her own attitude adjustment. It was starting again: the small panic attacks. She would have moments where her identity would seem as if it were slipping away and she barely knew what she wanted or who she was. She was strangely related to the Cohens and maybe what irritated her most about sitting in a room listening to Seth's grand ideas of Chrismukkah was that she would have to look at Sandy looking at Seth with that mix of awe and pride. She wished her dad would look at her that way — that he had reason to look at her that way. She couldn't believe Sandy Cohen was so strong. He was a man of morals and character. . . . most of all he was a great dad. No matter what had happened to Ryan, no matter how he had screwed up, goofed off, made a mess, or lost, when Sandy Cohen committed to being Ryan's legal guardian he stayed in the game. Marissa felt her stomach turn over as Sandy came down the stairs in his golf clothes; she wasn't sure if it was all envy or just a sadness that wrenched her apart. Why couldn't she find just one adult, just *one* to stand by her, too? Her mother was so critical and she had no right to be. Julie Cooper was an alligator in Prada shoes: a real fake. She knew her mother's past was a checkered flag of mishaps and somehow a powerful man with money always saved her. Marissa wanted something different for herself and hoped that someday there would be a man who would stand by her. She loved

Summer but having a girlfriend wasn't always like having a boyfriend — and she laughed to herself: She *should* know that!

Ryan never liked social gatherings, especially the ones where the caterers weren't involved. There was no anonymity when it was an intimate crowd. Every time there had been a quiet sitdown or social gathering it had ended with him and Caleb fighting. He sighed. Well, at least that wouldn't happen tonight. No one liked to talk about Caleb anymore. The scars ran too deep for everyone. Ryan was unsure he would like any plan that Seth came up with for Chrismukkah, especially one that now included "just family." He worried that Seth had lost perspective since his life had become so easygoing. He had become a ladies' man. He had earned his talent. It was almost better when Seth had been nervous and insecure: At least then his ego didn't explode into self-indulgent rants.

Ryan shook his head. He couldn't believe how angry and bitter he was feeling about everything. As if his past were clawing at his heels and taking over his mind. He watched Kirsten enter the room with her big Californian smile, white teeth, and pretty hair. He knew he was so lucky to gain a mom like Kirsten — at this point in his life — but the memory of his own past at Christmas was unshakable. He looked over at Marissa and smiled. She tilted her head slightly to the left and as she faked a smile back he could see the waver in her lip. He knew she'd had more than just a little schnapps on the way out the door.

He went and sat down next to her on the couch.

"You smell like a drunk peppermint patty," he said.

"Thanks, next time I'll drink the straw-berry schnapps and then I can smell like a drunk lollipop." Marissa stood up to move to another seat but Ryan grabbed her arm.

"If you move you'll have to sit next to your mother," he said.

In her slightly altered buzz she gave him a sloppy kiss on the forehead and sat down again.

"Thanks, I'll pretend we're getting along and stay right here."

It was the way she kissed him that made Ryan's mind slip into the past again. He looked over at Marissa with the afternoon sun shining across her face. She was washed out and tired and slumped slightly in the chair; with her hands folded over her chest, her eyes slightly watery from an alcoholic daze, she appeared to be a much younger version of his mother for a moment.

Ryan felt so sick he grabbed his stomach. Seth had told him a lot about things he talked about in therapy and Ryan knew that boys were often attracted to people who were like their mothers, but was that it? Had he always loved Marissa because he thought he might be able to save her? Did he love Marissa because he wanted more than anything to help her to stop drinking? The thought made his entire body shake.

"You okay, Ryan? You look like you've seen a ghost," she said.

"Maybe I should get some air." Ryan stood and realized everyone else had taken their seats.

Kirsten sat on the arm of a chair where she held Sandy's hand. Julie Cooper sat with her knees under her chin, cornered on one end of the couch, while Summer sat at the other end, rapidly bouncing her leg up and down.

"Come on, Cohen!" Summer snapped. "I want to get this scheming plan of yours over with so I can head to the mall and get even with my stepmonster." She looked over at Kirsten and Julie, who stared back in horror.

"Sorry. Things have been a little bumpy since my dad left for Liechtenstein or wherever."

"Ah, no, *mon cherie*. The night is young for us to uncover the true meaning of Chrismukkah," swooned Seth.

Ryan held his stomach and slid down the side of the chair, sitting at Marissa's feet.

"Okay, everyone. Here is the great Chrismukkah plan." Seth jumped on top of the coffee table. "The time has come to unveil the rewarding, undeniable brilliance of discovering the true meaning of Chrismukkah."

He paused. "No drumroll?" He stood disappointed by everyone's lack of enthusiasm.

Sandy began a small tap on the edge of the coffee table and smiled.

Marissa was sickened by his support of this Seth craziness — or deep down she felt the urge for a quick shot and knew she was jealous.

"Okay, 'tis the season with no reasons in the OC. This is a time for giving and caring and sharing of yourself, and for most of us we have known only the good things of life, except Dad of course at times and the few years that Mom put up with Dad . . . "

"Seth!" Kirsten warned in her kind, teasing voice. Marissa and Julie both rolled their eyes.

"Can we get on with this, Seth? I have an important appointment at the new Bliss West Coast," snapped Julie, standing up and smoothing out her sweatpants. Julie had lost a bit of herself since Caleb was gone. She dressed more often in Juicy Couture than haute and there were even times she preferred to paint her own nails than go out and face the crowds.

"I was so there and you cannot be late," interrupted Summer. "They are *so* uptight

East Coast, there is no way they will last out here."

"I know, they confirmed my appointment like three times on my cell," sighed Julie. "And then they emphasized I should be there fifteen minutes early. Fifteen minutes early? I thought to myself — this is the OC, it's not like I do much else. Sorry, Kirsten, not all of us run mega companies and still manage to spend time with our husbands and children."

Marissa was mortified.

"Julie, this is not the place to discuss our past business transactions," warned Kirsten.

"Right, of course. Caleb's old office would have been better." Julie sat back down and drew her legs up against her chest and kicked off her flip-flops. One flew right into Seth's hands.

"Does this mean I have the ball back in my court?" he asked.

"Go on, Seth," urged Sandy. "I think the natives are restless."

"Okay. So, as I was saying, here in the OC we know more brand names than charities and we spend more time on our wardrobes, gadgets, toys, and houses than on helping out. I have gathered you all here to participate in the great gift of real giving. This year the theme of Chrismukkah is to find the miracle in yourself by giving your time to others." Seth spread out his hand in a joyous moment of prayer.

"This year I want us to reach into our hearts and pull out the value of what we do best. We will not rest until we find that we are each capable of giving and receiving miracles." Seth had begun to stomp and slap his hands together like a Baptist minister.

"Uh, Seth, are we supposed to start screaming and saying amen?" said Ryan.

"No, but it's not a bad idea to get in

touch with your inner goodness and light. I was feeling a little more like Jesus on the mount or Moses leading his people. But this is about transcendence and the eight days of Hanukkah."

"The waaa?" asked Summer. "Does this have to do with those questions I asked The Nana two years ago?"

"Right you are, my sweet little Torah study, but this has to do with miracles."

"I think we need a miracle to get you to tell us the plan," sighed Marissa.

Seth sulked for a moment and put his hand across his chest, showing his hurt.

Ryan slapped him gently on the knee. "Come on, Seth, just let us know, man, without all the confusing stuff. You can explain it later to those of us who aren't Jewish."

He looked at Ryan and was happy; Ryan always knew how to change his mood. "Okay. Marissa, Ryan, Summer, and myself" — he pointed in each person's direction — "are going to work for you," and he pointed to Julie, Kirsten, and Sandy.

"But there are four of us and only three adults."

"Right now there are three but tomorrow Jimmy Cooper will be home to see his family and can lead one stray misfit through the ropes of being Santa's little helper."

"So that is the great plan?" Summer screamed. "We get to be Santa's little helper and wrap presents and run errands for those four while we should be taking a rest after exams and gearing up for a major New Year's Eve party?"

"Ahh, Summer harbors the soul of giving," sighed Sandy.

"Actually, Summer, it's a little more complicated than that. As we give ourselves for the eight days of Hanukkah, the adults must give us their real time and attention."

"Right, like any one of them has spent more than eight hours with us for the last six months," snarled Marissa.

"Exactly the point, Princess of Drunkenness, I mean Darkness."

Marissa stuck her tongue out at Seth.

"This is why we're giving our time to them. They are bestowing their gifts of life's most precious lessons upon us, and all of it shall be done for eight days to celebrate the miracle of Hanukkah and the real job of being Santa's little helper."

"I'm confused," said Marissa, truly dazed.

"I'll explain it to you later when you are a little more willing to listen."

"I am willing to listen. I just don't like this time of year, and why should I? Give me one good reason why I should love

Christmas. It is one extended reminder that my life fell apart and the entire season is all about a family that I don't have and doesn't exist anymore."

Silence fell over the room. For all of their differences, Ryan knew just how Marissa felt.

Then Sandy smiled at Marissa. "You're right, and this is often a very depressing time of year. It always seems to bring up our oldest wounds and because the pace rarely allows us the time we need to grieve for the ghosts of Christmas or Hanukkah past."

Both Ryan and Marissa stared at him with awe. Kirsten placed her hand on his knee, and even Julie Cooper cast her eyes to the ground. As happy and fun as the holy days were, everyone knew it had been a long year and it was true there were times it felt like they wanted to skip the entire process.

"So does everyone understand the rules?"

"Not exactly," sighed Summer. "No gifts? Is that what you are really saying here? No TSE cashmere? Wolford stockings? Diesel? Dior? Hermès? Dolce & Gabbana? And most of all, no Christian Louboutin four-inch stiletto with clear plastic Perspex heels?"

"I thought Perspex was already out?" Julie said.

"Mom, you are way too old to be wearing clear plastic stilettos. You'll look like a porn star."

Julie flashed Marissa a warning glare not to embarrass her any further but it was clear Marissa didn't need to embarrass her mother; Julie Cooper had done a fine job all by herself. Marissa was mortified by the unending scandals her mother provided for Newport Beach. It was a sad burden to live with, but at least her father knew when to get out of town. Sometimes she wished her mother would disappear and she could start over in a place where no one knew her past.

Seth cleared his throat. "Okay, here are the rules: Every day during our vacation we show up for work with whomever our assigned adult is. It is our job to figure out what we can share and our mentor's job to find ways we can actually be helpful while learning something. There will be no gifts given. This year it is all about trying to outdo one another with the real meaning of Christmas and Hanukkah. For those of you who have forgotten what that means, *Summer*, it is about giving and creating miracles every day."

Kirsten raised her hand.

"Yes, Mom."

"Well, Seth, this is an extremely important time of year for me. I have a large charity event, and the ball is on Christmas

Eve this year. If I am supposed to host a young mentor, I need to know they are really here to help. What's my guarantee?"

Seth was perplexed. He hadn't thought that anyone would slack off but as he looked around the room he realized there was a very good chance it could happen.

"I suggest a little friendly competition," offered Sandy. "At the end of the week whomever we felt has learned the most, given the most, and derived the true meaning of Chrismukkah out of his or her service will be able to pick a charity and we will donate an undisclosed amount of money to it."

Kirsten gave Sandy a soft kiss on the cheek. "That's a wonderful idea. I guess you can take the boy out of the Bronx but not the Bronx out of the boy. I'm in." She turned to Julie. "And you, Julie?"

"Sure, sure. I'm in. I'm just not exactly clear on what my talents are." Julie realized the room was silent because everyone had drawn the same conclusion.

Seth couldn't take it anymore. It was agonizing to watch everyone withdraw from his great idea of finding the true meaning of sharing in the holidays. Basically he had just saved them thousands of dollars in gift giving and harried lines and lotteries to get their hands on the portable PlayStation of the moment.

"Okay, adults, ante up your cell phones."

Julie clutched hers to her chest, Sandy held his out, and Kirsten quickly checked her messages.

"Come on — everyone put a cell phone in the Christmas stocking." Seth took the phones and shook them gently. He held the fur-lined stocking out to Ryan.

"Pick one. Don't be afraid. Any one will do."

Ryan felt the smooth edges of each

phone. Each one would bring a very different meaning to the next eight days. He knew Sandy probably didn't have a flip phone — too metrosexual for him — so he held on to the one that felt like it was a solid Nokia.

He looked up at Seth.

"Don't show it, bro. Keep your hand down."

Marissa picked next. She could feel two small flip phones and one was definitely still warm. She imagined it was her mother's. It was the one thing Julie Cooper held close to her at all times. She moved to the cooler one and took it.

"No peeking," warned Seth.

Ahh, Summer. No matter how angry she seemed, it made Seth want to kiss her. Her lip stuck out like a spoiled child's and it was clear she would have been happier running laps through the mall than working for eight days to help someone else.

"Go ahead. You hold the key."

"Why don't you pick?" she challenged him.

"Well, I thought since I am the mastermind of Chrismukkah it is essential that I am here to light the candles, help everyone understand the goal for the day, and since Jimmy will be staying with us it makes perfect sense that he and I can work on our extracurricular activities together."

"What activities?" snapped Ryan. "Isn't it enough we are giving you our holiday break after a grueling semester and exams?"

"Huh — real Chrismukkah cheer. Thanks for the support."

"I thought it might be fun to make some gingerbread houses and try to do some crafts, okay? I mean, Martha Stewart can't be the only person in the world who knows how to use a hot-glue gun," Ryan replied sarcastically.

"Oh, I always wanted to make a gingerbread house!" Kirsten smiled, either missing his tone or deciding to ignore it.

"Ryan, I hope you got Kirsten — maybe you can give her some cooking classes," chuckled Sandy.

Seth stepped back and waved his hands like he was performing a magic trick.

"I now officially invite you to participate in the eight days of Chrismukkah and discover the true meaning of the season. You may look at your phones."

Marissa held up the black flip phone she had picked.

Sandy jumped up and gave her a hug. "Well, Marissa, it looks like you'll be learning a little about the law! That is great. I have some really heavy cases starting in the new year and I need to make sure we put the files in order before everyone runs off to the Caribbean for the holidays. It will be great to have your help."

Marissa couldn't believe the way Sandy hugged her. It felt so genuine and warm. As if he really believed she could do something more than look pretty.

Ryan was surprised that he hadn't picked Sandy's phone. The one he selected was a single silver Motorola where the mouthpiece slid down.

Julie Cooper let out a shocked groan that sounded as if she had been kicked in the stomach.

Ryan's own groan matched it. Julie shrugged her shoulders and looked at Seth. "Exactly what should I do with him?"

"That, my dear neighbor, is your job to figure out."

Ryan put his palms over his forehead and rubbed his temples.

Julie sighed. "You think you have a headache now? Just wait."

Kirsten looked at Summer.

"I guess that means we are together

through the annual New Playgrounds for Needy Neighbors ball and fund-raiser. I guess I could use some extra hands."

Kirsten wasn't the last person Summer would have picked but it felt strange that she was going to spend the next eight days palling around with Seth's mom. A little too cute for her taste.

Seth flopped down on the couch and placed a hand on Summer's knee. This was dangerous territory since things had been so rocky between them but he liked the idea of Summer and his mother palling around. It was so very cute and daughter-in-law-like.

Summer wrinkled her nose and shook her head, just shaking her perfect hair loose slightly.

"Don't go there, Seth. It ain't going to happen."

Seth rubbed his hands together. "Of course not, Summer — but I do wonder why you already feel uncomfortable about it." He smiled that devilish grin and Summer excused herself. Everyone took this as their cue to make their way back to their rooms and houses, lost in the idea of what they could actually give someone else without buying it.

THE OC

3

Summer arrived at Kirsten's office shortly before nine A.M. She was sure that Kirsten would be on time and she wanted to make a good impression. She felt a bit of a burden having Seth's mom as her guide through this exercise. It seemed she and Kirsten had never really had much to say to each other and that Kirsten had always preferred Anna, Seth's previous girlfriend, because she was artistic and smart and clever. Summer didn't really count Alex — that relationship had been short and weird.

It was always clear that Summer would spend most of her life being a corporate wife, not a mogul. Summer knew she was smart enough, but she also had to work for it. She wasn't like those girls who could just absorb everything and never take notes. School was hard work and nothing she wanted to extend forever. The sooner she felt she could settle into a good marriage, the better off she would be — of course, finding a man her father liked would be the hardest part. No one was ever good enough for Summer. She laughed at the memory of the first time Seth had met her father. Seth had been such a nervous wreck that he chattered all through the meal and barely let anyone else say a word. It was awkward and horrible . . . and so funny. At least Kirsten and Sandy had always made their home welcoming. They were like that. The kind of parents who never minded finding Seth and his friends in the living room or out by the pool. They seemed to relish the company and who knew why they took on so much trouble. Summer knew that for all the talent her own father had, the one thing he didn't do well was give his time away for charity. He was noble enough that he had done a lot of work on children without money but when it came down to his free time, he would rather be on the golf course. Summer knew he lived by his scalpel and his driver.

Summer flipped the pages of an architectural magazine. She really did like to imagine what her own house would be like someday and was always impressed by modern designs like those Frank Lloyd Wright had created. In her father's library there was a collection of books that Summer had loved to look through as a little girl; the photos of Fallingwater and Taliesen were the most moving. She liked to flip through the pages because they gave her a sense of calm. When things got out of control, even now she would go and just stare at the pictures of those houses until she felt better. Seth had once made fun of her because he said it was "not a Summer move." She had felt really defensive.

"I am not all about lipstick, you know," she had said to him.

"I know, beautiful, but Frank Lloyd Wright? I mean, what do you want to do, be an architect?"

"I never thought about what I want to do. They just make me feel better."

"I thought Manolo Blahnik high-heeled mules and milk shakes made you feel better?"

"That, too, but Manolo is a real artist."

"Summer, let's be clear here. I am the artist and you are the fashion plate. I need you to look good or I don't look good."

At the time she had believed it was a compliment but now she found herself starting to wonder about Seth. He seemed to forget how hard she worked in school and always cut her down just a little bit when she made a mistake in class. He dwelled more on the idea that she should work in fashion than she did. There were times she missed Zach and his seriousness.

Argh! She pinched herself on the leg. *What has happened to me?* she thought. *Ever since Cohen came into my life I worry about people being attracted to me for my brain? HELLLLOOOOO? Not necessary.* She thought she might feel better if she went and looked at the cute business outfit she had worn to be Kirsten's assistant. She had on great Wolford knee-highs, a cute Gucci Catholic schoolgirl skirt, Christian Dior Chinese slippers, and a short-sleeve TSE cashmere sweater. She stepped just far enough back from the glass that she could see her reflection. She did look great here in the office, very professional and like a really cool advertisement for dressing for Fridays in *Glamour* magazine. As she turned to check if her butt was causing the pleats in the skirt to kick up too much to the rear, Kirsten entered, frenzied and on the phone.

"I just don't think it is the right concept," she snapped. "We need clean, fast, and energy-efficient. You are trying to pass off on me something fluffy, indirect, and labor-intensive."

Summer had never heard Kirsten sound so tough. Her shocked face was obviously noted because Kirsten feigned a quick friendly smile.

"Just sit down," barked Kirsten.

Shocked by the new woman she saw before her, Summer buckled and sat on the edge of the couch. Summer had always imagined Kirsten as some kind of pushover. Kirsten was so full of love and had endured so much humiliation from her own dad, Summer thought there was nothing that really ruffled Kirsten's feathers. But today Kirsten looked tough and hard. Summer imagined that after all those years of cleaning up Caleb's messes maybe Kirsten was a lot tougher than anyone knew. And yet Kirsten looked cool, really in control, and kind of sexy. Of course, Summer meant it in the way that sexy is for women who are totally on the ball, like Demi Moore and all of the new Charlie's Angels.

Kirsten looked over at Summer, who was perched at the end of the chair like a little bird waiting for food.

"No, darling, not you," she said in a completely different tone, then back into the phone in a frank direct voice, "Just sit down and think it over and don't come back to me without being ready to meet my needs." Then she hung up.

"Sorry about that. I just hate being given the run-around. It is an endless story once you're a woman in business." She smiled. "Oh, I'm probably not making any sense."

"No, it's cool. Totally cool."

"Totally? OC talk or Valley?"

"Simply serene?"

"Better vocabulary. People take you much more seriously if they can't understand a word you're saying. It's a great trick to have up your sleeve as a woman. A good vocabulary is like showing you have a vault of information and they shouldn't take advantage of you." Kirsten slammed her fist on the table.

"Wow. That must have been a lousy phone call."

Kirsten let out an exasperated sigh. "Well, Summer, things have been pretty bumpy since everything went wrong around my dad. Sometimes I feel I haven't recovered and at the same time people are demanding so much more of me." She sighed again. "I do love my Seth but this isn't the best timing. I need every minute of my day to plan the National Charity League's Christmas Eve auction fund-raiser and I feel a little guilty that I don't have time to be a better mentor."

Summer thought for a minute. Did Kirsten Cohen, the citadel of all families in the OC, need some ego buffing? Did Kirsten Cohen, the woman who every other mother emulated, really need help?

"Hey, Ms. C, don't sweat it. I already learned two things today I could use."

"Summer, it's only twenty after nine. What could I have taught you by mouthing off?"

"Well, you just said a great way to have people give you more respect is by showing them you have a powerful vocabulary and that you are smarter than you look. I'm not that great at remembering dates and numbers but it's funny, I always remember the roots of words and do really well on vocabulary tests. I'm going to try and use them now more often in conversation."

Kirsten nodded. "Great — what else?"

"Well . . ." Summer thought this was going to sound really silly — no, *ridiculous* was a better word — no, *childish, insane, impractical, harebrained*! She chuckled. "Well Ms. C, I've never seen you be so tough and it gave me a lot of energy. As if suddenly . . . I thought it would be very interesting to run a business instead of being married to one."

Kirsten held her arms out and took Summer in them. When she pulled away, Ms. C looked a little blurry in the eyes.

"Thanks, Summer. Sometimes I have to say that though I feel like I run the business, I'm also married to it."

"Well, better than having nothing to do

but paint your toes and lie by the pool like my stepmonster." She shrugged.

"Lying by the pool sounds like a great idea to me right now."

"Well, we could always have an early lunch and pretend we're Europeans! That is what Coop and I do when things get rough. We just make an expensive reservation and go out for some power-lunch girl time." Summer covered her mouth in shock. She had forgotten to whom she was speaking — after all, Kirsten was a professional and now Summer was suggesting slacking off — on her first day!

"Well — if we get enough done maybe we can do just that. Don't look so shocked, Summer. As you get older, believe me, you realize that some days it pays to slack off," Kirsten said with a smile.

"But for now I need to introduce you to the major project we have. Okay. Let's get on the ball. The first thing I need you to do is:

1) Check that the flowers are grouped into sets of twelve for each table of twelve.
2) Double-check the master list of acceptances to the event with the running list.
3) At the end of every day, go by the receptionist and gather the new names that need to be added to the list.
4) Compare all of these names with the checks they've written for their seats and how many they are buying.
5) Double-check that the caterers have all green and white accessories and that the six trees I have on order will be adorned with only white ornaments.

6) The receptionist has a master list of teachers from the surrounding schools. I'd like you to keep calling them today, throughout the day, and maybe in the evening, too, to see if we can get any of them to agree to come to the fund-raiser and talk about why kids need new playgrounds."

"Uh, Ms. C?" stuttered Summer.

"Yes? Too fast? Too much?" Kirsten smiled.

"I don't know why kids need new playgrounds."

"This is a fund-raiser to begin building safe playgrounds in needy neighborhoods. I mean Chino, Riverside, Pomona. Places like that are not exactly our closest neighbors but they have a terrible problem with their playgrounds and need new materials that can withstand heavy rain without rusting, cracking, or chipping. Currently there are thousands of playgrounds that aren't safe because of toxic lead paint that was mixed into the color for outdoor use and durability, as well as the metals themselves that are high in lead. Many more have splintering wood and rickety chains. Also, without good ground coverage the kids can get seriously hurt — and most of them don't have health insurance. A trip to the emergency room can mean serious financial hardship. If we can generate enough money, we will be able to lay down recycled rubber matting to prevent injuries from falls as well. The average playground costs $150,000 and we want to replace up to twenty of them. That's a lot to raise."

"Wow. That sounds like a great cause. What are you auctioning off?"

Kirsten's face went pale.

"Is it a secret auction?" asked Summer.

Kirsten shook her head violently from one side to the other.

"No, it's not a secret auction?" Summer was really confused by Ms. C's behavior.

Ms. C placed her hands into her palms and started to breathe heavily.

"I think you need that long lunch now, Ms. C. Are you okay?"

"Oh, Summer, I can't tell you what I've done. I just forgot. I plain old forgot. I never forget." Kirsten Cohen looked like she was going to cry or be very ill.

"Forgot what?"

"I don't know what we are auctioning. I have been so busy planning this entire thing, getting in touch with local congress-men and civic leaders so that I could find out who really needed a new playground, and then the plates and the menu and the guest lists and not to mention everything else that's been going on . . . oh, Summer, what have I done? I need to raise close to three million dollars and I don't even have a plan."

Summer took a deep breath. She did sometimes wonder how adults managed to look so good on the outside when really they were just like kids on the inside. With all their lists and secretaries, this was basically like forgetting you had a midterm exam and then cramming for it the night before.

"I wish I could talk it over with Princess Sparkle," said Summer, somewhat disappointed in Kirsten. She'd seemed wickedly together just minutes before and now she was falling apart.

"Who is Princess Sparkle? . . . I mean she's not a therapist."

"Well, she sort of is. Princess Sparkle is like Captain Oats."

Kirsten rolled her eyes. Summer was not going to let Ms. C make fun of her. As far as she was concerned, Ms. C had just wiped out hard on the half slope and Summer was not impressed — or going to listen to any of it.

"When I talk to Princess Sparkle, and Seth talks to Captain Oats, we get a chance to work through things without judgment. It's a time we talk to someone who always listens to us and never gives us anything but support — even if it is imaginary. When I say we need a Princess Sparkle, I mean that we need a place that is safe for you to think of a good idea because you rubbed yourself into a White-out position."

"I used to talk to my Barbies," sighed Kirsten. "Well, actually, I talked to Pan Am Barbie."

"Pan What?"

"Kind of like Jet Blue Barbie? She was a stewardess. I used to take her out and talk to her when I felt really sad or upset. I always felt like she was so together in her little outfit and when things got rough for her she could just take off and fly around the world. She was so cool and had this awesome little pink suitcase and a little tray with coffee on it. I haven't thought of that in years."

"Well, where is she?" Summer asked.

"Oh, I don't know. My basement, somewhere between my yearbook, my security blanket, and my first prom dress. I had a huge collection but I think they're all gone."

"Too bad, Ms. C. Barbie is so hot right now."

"What do you mean, Summer?"

"Oh, you know, Barbie has it all together again. We love Barbie. She has the body, the man, the clothes, the cool, rocking music, a jamming Web site, fashion chic, and now she even has a posse called Cali Girl to hang out with at the beach."

"I thought Barbie was for, for, for . . ."

"For little girls?" asked Summer. "Sure. I mean, Barbie is for little girls, but did you know she even has her own fashion magazine? It's a total fashion monthly. When Barbie had her fiftieth anniversary, the women went nuts. I mean, you can buy and sell Barbies for thousands of dollars. I know someone who bid on the Jacqueline Kennedy Onassis Barbie for like two hundred thousand dollars or something *nutty — I mean crazy — no, outlandish, outrageous, eccentric, bizarre. . . .*"

"What about old Barbies?" asked Kirsten.

"Oh, they are the best. The real deal pulls in major coin. My stepmonster won't touch anything but Chanel and yet if she sees a tag sale with Barbies for sale she digs like a coal miner."

"But aren't they ruined?"

"Ms. C, didn't you play with their hair?

And their clothes? It's a makeover Stepford Wife style."

"Summer — I think you are absolutely right. We need two things right now."

"What about my list?"

"Tomorrow. Right now we need to call the radio stations and get the word out that we are looking for Barbies to be donated for the New Playgrounds for Needy Neighbors fund-raiser. Call every woman on our guest list and ask her to go down in her basement and pull them out and donate them for the cause."

"Then what?" asked Summer, a little bit confused.

"You are going to work doing your best Barbie makeovers and then we are auctioning them off to the highest bidder! Come on — you can help me think up a good commercial on the way over to the studio. We'll use your voice because it's younger."

Summer squealed. This was going to be an awesome week. Not only were she and Ms. C going to play Barbie dress-up but she — Summer Roberts — was about to star in her own radio commercial! She could just kiss Seth Cohen for being so brilliant — then again she should kiss herself for being so brilliant — *no, inspired, skillful, gifted, clever. . . .*

THE

4

Marissa stood at the door to Sandy Cohen's law office and took a deep breath. She looked out at the beach and wondered if she should just turn and walk down into the horizon. What could she do for Sandy Cohen? She felt inadequate already. She hated when this feeling came over her. She knew that the next feeling would be a longing for a drink. It was as if the feelings lived together. First came insecurity, inadequacy, and fear and moving right along beside them the devil on her shoulder who would whisper that a drink would help calm her down. She knew that everyone was swapping prescription drugs and it would be safe to say she'd nail anything from Xanax to Prozac or pop a few Paxil instead, but she didn't like pills. She laughed. It was always hard for her to swallow stuff as a child. Even now, she liked baby aspirin instead of taking a few Tylenol for her headache.

Marissa placed her hand on the doorknob and turned it. It was locked. She saw windows open between the blinds that flapped gently in the breeze but the door itself was locked. She sighed with relief. Maybe Sandy had forgotten. It was typical, she thought, *Once again Marissa is forgotten.* It pained her to feel left behind by her father and ignored by her mother. Only her sister seemed to know how she felt, and when she called from boarding school Marissa had to admit she was a bit jealous. Her sister at least had gotten a fresh start.

Marissa leaned on the banister and wondered how long she should wait. Was this like the teacher rules at school? You waited five minutes, then made a list of everyone who attended the class, then after fifteen minutes you brought the list to the attendance secretary and took a free period. How long should she wait for Sandy Cohen? She realized she didn't even have his cell phone number. She flipped open her phone to call Seth and then thought again.

If she didn't call that meant she didn't have an answer and not having an answer was an easier way of bluffing later. If she knew the rules, she would have to play by them. If she didn't know the rules . . . well, then, everything was a viable line of defensive reasoning. A few hours on the beach could be blamed on Sandy's lateness and not her reluctance to stay in an office with him all day. She squinted into the sun and thought about slipping over to Peet's to get a coffee.

As she made her way down the steps onto the sand to walk along the beach, a surfer blocked her way.

"Hey, Marissa, you're early."

When she looked up, Sandy Cohen was smiling at her with his hair dripping wet and a small cut on his cheek.

"I was thinking about getting us some coffee to start the day." She smiled.

Sandy raised his large eyebrows and pressed his lips together. "Funny, you don't know how I take my coffee. Are you sure you weren't about to bolt?" He laughed.

Marissa was appalled. Was that what made Sandy Cohen a good parent? He was a mind reader?

He slapped his wet hand on her back and shook his head, pushing her back toward the office.

"Marissa. After years of selecting juries, years of staring down delinquents, cons, and dealers, I have learned the difference between someone who is telling the truth, a liar, and a darn good liar. You, my dear, are a bad liar." He laughed hard as he dug out the key to his office from his wet surf trunks.

Marissa felt ashamed. Her lies never made her feel ashamed. Maybe because it seemed her mother would rather believe them than know the truth.

"Sorry, Mr. Cohen," she mumbled.

"It's okay, Marissa, if I lived in your house I'd lie, cheat, or steal just to get out the door in the morning." Sandy threw his crusty surfboard on the couch.

Marissa looked around the office. It was a large, comfortable, outstanding mess of papers, boxes with black marker scribbled on the sides, take-out food containers, and computer wires.

"Sorry about the office," he said. "Every

time I try and get organized or clean it up there is a crisis. You know what I mean?"

Actually Marissa knew just what he meant. If it hadn't been for Summer, Seth, and Ryan, she would have never moved out of her father's house. Crises seemed to follow her everywhere.

"I guess we're all good at crisis management," she said with a smile.

"Yes. It's a specialty here in Newport — everything from business to charities. Always with billions of dollars and billions of crises to build on." For a moment Sandy felt bad about including his wife in that group — even by implication. He knew she was still going through so much since all that had happened with her father but he couldn't help it.

"Sometimes, Marissa, a few cons and some car busts seem like heaven by comparison to embezzlement, foreign bank accounts, and blackmail."

Sandy ran his fingers through his hair and realized that wasn't exactly what he wanted to say, either. Now he felt bad about dishing about Ryan and his brother.

"Marissa . . ."

She looked up at him.

"I'm going to change and then we'll go get coffee together. Then somehow you'll try and help me manage all these boxes and hopefully by the end of the week you'll get my sense of humor — which is basically all I have left at the end of every day."

She nodded.

Sandy slipped upstairs and she could hear the shower turn on. The office reminded her of the beach shack where she had lived with her girlfriend, Alex. Alex had taught her so much about living on her own. She was sad she could never really love Alex in a way that meant they could have a life together, but Marissa knew her heart belonged elsewhere.

However, she was grateful for the deeper level of friendship that Alex had taught her — and of course the basic lessons in home management. Marissa began to slowly walk through the office collecting take-out containers and placing them in a soggy garbage bag.

Funnily enough, it reminded her of living with her dad during the divorce. She had loved the days when they ordered food in and sat on the couch watching old reruns of sporting events. She missed the simplicity of his small apartment. It seemed funny to say but she would trade the mansion, the pool, the large walk-in closets, most of her wardrobe, hundreds of shoes, and her life of endless cash flow for the simple days she spent sitting on the couch with her dad when he was broke. Money, it seemed, had always made her life more complicated than easy. Money made people jealous, mean, and cruel. The days she had spent with her dad, broke and quietly talking, or the times she and Alex just stayed in and lit candles, were some of her happiest memories of the past few years. Money, it seemed, made people too busy for one another. They were always rushing here and there to make appointments: for manicures, haircuts, shoe sales, and things that probably didn't make a world of difference outside the OC.

Sandy put a cool hand on her shoulder. "I called your name three times. What are you thinking about?" he asked.

"Well . . . actually, I was thinking about things that matter here in the OC that probably do not matter anywhere else. Like who cares if I have the Versace pajamas or a Hermès Birkin and, well, money." She wrinkled her nose.

"Great. Already you're thinking like a public defender and you've only been at work ten minutes." He laughed. "Want some coffee?"

"Definitely, but I have to say we need to get these containers cleaned up because I can't concentrate in this frat house."

"What? This is Jewish cuisine. There is a whole culture behind Jewish take-out."

"I just thought it was because Kirsten can't cook." She laughed. "Not that anyone can here — at least not without their personal chef and nutritionist."

"Which really is beyond the point because they'll just get any excess sucked out or tucked up by Summer's father." Sandy chuckled and threw a carton in the bag like he was playing basketball.

"Hey, watch out. That was almost the soy sauce dry-cleaning special."

"Okay — put the garbage can in the center of the room and we'll see how many we can each get in. After we're done with the take-out we can move on to those files."

They moved around the room imitating great basketball stars and throwing random items into the wastebasket. Marissa stripped off her Stuart Weitzman heels and was amazed at how well she did dashing past the basket and dunking things in — granted, the basket was on the floor so she couldn't get too excited, but she thought a lot about all those basketball games from the seventies she and her dad had watched.

"Hey, that looked like a move by Dr. J!" Sandy said.

"You mean Julius Winfield Erving the second?" She laughed.

"Way to go, kid. I didn't think you were old enough to know who that is."

"I'm not. You know my dad was a fan of the oldies. I probably know more about

the 76ers than I do about World War Two."
She smiled.

Sandy nodded. "I miss your dad," he said.

Marissa looked up and felt a sharp pain in her chest. No one ever talked about missing her dad.

"But, I mean, well, you're a man, a guy — I mean, guys don't miss guys, do they?"

"Ahh, another great thing about being Jewish is that I don't have to pretend to be all macho. We're huggers and kissers. I'm a sappy guy. Come on, I'm Seth's dad — where do you think he got it? Kirsten? Caleb?"

"I guess I thought I was the only one who ever thought about my dad." She shrugged, drawing a boat in the dust on the desktop.

"We all think about him, but I really miss having a friend. There was no one like him for me. He just knew how to laugh at the OC when things got too hot. I needed that."

Marissa looked up at Sandy, who suddenly looked tired, and she felt he had just said something she knew but never could put into words. Her dad, Jimmy, really knew how to laugh.

Sandy lunged at her and Marissa jumped backward, shocked.

"Hey, that is very expensive dust. I can't have you start cleaning it up without the proper breakfast. I'm a starved surfer and you look like you haven't eaten in days. Let's take a walk and talk before we start working." He opened the door.

"And cleaning!" she sighed.

"When did you become such a neat freak?" asked Sandy as they walked along the boardwalk.

"I guess it was when I lived with Alex. I learned that I had to take care of myself and there was no maid, no one to help me, no one to vacuum or mop the floors, and one day our apartment was so filthy and covered with sticky surfaces that I just thought if I didn't do it myself I'd be sick."

"Good thinking." Sandy waved to a few surfers just coming off the water.

"The strange part was that once I did it myself I felt really good. I didn't have to wait for my laundry. I knew how to separate the clothes and when I wanted something I washed it. Okay, I admit ironing is not my forte." She laughed at the time she burned a hole through three shirts because she thought she could iron them all at once. To make it easier she just laid them on top of one another.

"It feels good to know you can make it by yourself?" asked Sandy.

"Yeah, I guess. Only I didn't really make it. I mean, I was a lousy cook and, well, you know Alex and I didn't really have a permanent thing but she was like my best friend. I mean, not that anyone can replace Summer."

They walked up to an outdoor café that Marissa had never been to before. She had wanted to try it but always thought the crowd looked too old for her. Sandy pulled out a chair and motioned for her to sit.

"I love this place. I can see the water, I can get the gossip, and I can order the Hungry Surfer Breakfast with egg whites, turkey bacon, low-fat hollandaise sauce, and mixed greens. Down at the Jersey Shore the Hungry Surfer is two pounds of grease and you're lucky if you find the egg or the bacon, and they think hollandaise is a place people wear wooden shoes."

Marissa smiled and kept her hand away from her mouth.

"Ah, now I can see you are finally starting to relax," said Sandy.

"What do you mean?"

"Well, you finally stopped covering your mouth."

"My therapist once noticed that. . . . I mean . . . well, you know I had to see someone."

"Marissa, you never have to apologize or make excuses around me, okay?" Sandy watched her until she finally nodded back. "Good," he said, rubbing his hands together. "So tell me what you are good at," said Sandy. She wasn't sure what was more shocking: that she couldn't think of what she was good at, or that he seemed genuinely interested.

"I don't really know. I mean, that first time I lived away it helped me figure out how to do things on my own. I almost envy my sister for being at boarding school because she's really learning how to be independent."

"Marissa, we all have natural talents. I remember when I was a little boy my mother used to say: 'Sandy, I don't want to argue about this one. One day you'll grow up and take it to the high court but for now you just take it to bed!' I always knew I was cut out to pick a fight with someone."

"I just never thought about it, I guess."

"Well, from where I sit, you're great at events. You're always the person in charge of creating themes, organizing everyone to get together, making sure all the details are in place," said Sandy.

"I never really thought about it that way. I like that, but actually what I enjoy most is convincing the committee my ideas are right on target. Remember the Snow Ball? The head of school was totally against all that ice and snow and it turned out to be one of the most successful events I ever did. People still talk about the ice slide and sculptures."

"So you feel pretty creative, too? You like coming up with themes?"

"I guess. I like finding a way to make it all work — not necessarily working it all out. Does that make sense?"

"Sounds like you'll be a good lawyer's assistant!"

"I don't know anything about the law, though."

"You know the difference between right and wrong." Sandy raised an eyebrow.

"Sometimes."

"Well, that's all you need to know to start. A good backbone and some idea that life can be unfair. And that, my dear, I think you certainly know!"

Sandy placed his hand on her head and messed up her hair, shaking her head like a mop.

"And by the way — we are a casual law office. No need to show up looking like 'Jacqueline Kennedy goes to the beach,' okay?"

Marissa kicked off her heels and let

her toes run over the bumpy surface of the boardwalk. The sun had warmed the wooden planks under her feet and she realized that for the first time in months she felt safe to be herself.

5

Ryan would have preferred swimming in shark-infested waters, or dancing at another cotillion, rather than spending eight uninterrupted days with Julie Cooper. Things with him and Julie had never gone well. Why? Julie should have been Ryan's biggest supporter. She had been born and raised in Riverside, just a short distance from Chino but even farther along on the way to nowhere land. Growing up, Ryan had thought Riverside was pretty cool. They had nicer parks and the reservoirs where kids could hang out and be rowdy without getting into trouble with the cops. The best party he had ever been to was over Julie's way by Mockingbird Canyon. He had thought it was relaxed and cool the way everyone just pulled their cars up to the empty field and turned on the lights as the sun went down. There seemed to be less crime there even though the kids in Riverside were not rich by any means, but they seemed . . . happier being from trailer parks and broken homes. In Chino, where he grew up, the kids were always angry and waiting to bust out with their fists.

Ryan had to admit that Julie Cooper had assimilated into the life of the very rich with ease. The women from Chino were always being called baby-makers, while Julie Cooper was definitely a husband-taker. He had often thought that it was amazing how she was able to move among the wealthy while he struggled to find a balance. He knew she had more years of practice, but he was always surprised by how entitled she felt to all of the luxuries she had. Especially things she hadn't worked for but had married into. The entire situation with Caleb had been surprising — and appalling — to everyone. But somehow Julie Cooper managed to make it seem completely natural, as if it were her very right to have it all.

Ryan was supposed to meet Julie at a storage unit to sort out her stuff. He was surprised when he pulled up to find her already waiting, dressed in an old T-shirt and jeans.

Ryan took a deep breath and stepped out of the car no backing out now.

"You're here," Julie said, sounding surprised.

Ryan nodded.

"Well, come on. We have a lot of work to do." She unlocked the shed and raised the door.

Ryan followed her into a large, cluttered space. The storage unit was huge — and filled except for a space in the middle. He looked around at the boxes piled high in every corner, and newspapers and bubble wrap draped all over the floor.

"I want to clear this place out. Some of this stuff I want to use in my new place, but some of it can just go."

Don't you need a web as well? thought Ryan.

"Some of it is *me*, my style, my colors, my life. But a lot of it doesn't fit."

"And do you want me to build you a coffin to sleep in during the day?" Ryan had meant to keep the comment to himself but it had slipped out loud and clear.

Julie stared at him in distaste. "How can you stay so close-minded after you've walked the line between living in poverty and being the suddenly adopted son to some of the richest people in California?"

"I don't think about the money. I think about the way people care for me."

Julie rolled her eyes. "Ah, how sweet of you. I'll tell you something — you should think about the money."

"Is there anything else you think about?" he asked.

Julie looked past Ryan's shoulder as if she saw a ghost and her own face began to lose its rich color. Her eyes glazed over and she sighed.

"I don't like to think about anything else, Ryan."

Her eyes moved from the shadows on the wall to his. "If I only think about the money, I don't have to think about the past. You should know what I mean."

For just a moment Ryan felt his heart break for the snake in Julie Cooper, because he knew exactly what she meant.

"So, Ryan, I thought you might give me some help. I know you are good at construction — destruction, too — but I do not need a demolition crew here. Actually I don't really want anybody here right now. But I *do* need someone who can help me get all these old boxes, papers, and junk out. So what do you say?"

Ryan actually felt relieved. He was unsure what he could do for Julie, and the idea that she wanted to move and reorganize, was something concrete he knew he was capable of.

"Sure. I'm also good at basic carpentry, construction, and painting. Definitely some of my talents."

"Well, the only skills I need," Julie replied, "is some miracle. You can spare me the rest."

Ryan looked down at the floor. He was sure he deserved this, but it still hurt.

Julie paused as if about to speak, but instead gestured at some boxes. "Let's start here."

As they began to work, Julie's mind wandered. *No one ever lets you forget, do they? Even this kid from Chino. His every look seemed like a rebuke. I've spent years trying to erase my past only to have it rise up from the sea and crush my dreams like a tidal wave. But you get stronger. And one day when people snicker behind your back, you're able to turn around and make sure they laugh in your face. No matter how strong you become, the snide comments always sting.*

Ryan glanced at Julie, surprised to feel a slight stab of pity. She looked small and vulnerable standing there surrounded by these remnants of her past life. This wasn't the polished, brittle Julie Cooper he was used to. The woman who stood in front of him in a dirty old rock-'n'-roll T-shirt and worn jeans was raw, unfinished, hurt, and capable of things no one gave her credit for.

"Okay, why don't we get to work?" he said cautiously.

"Fine. I want to go through most of the boxes slowly and figure out what to keep or not. Start moving these boxes into a clear spot so I can do that."

Ryan shrugged. Being good at physical labor felt more like a burden than a joy right now. He wanted to be like Seth and have a brain that incorporated many things at once. Maybe then he'd know how to handle the next few days.

Julie peeked into one of the boxes. She picked up a box that was too large for her and stumbled. Ryan caught it as she fell backward onto a black leather couch.

"I hate this couch," she said. "This is the next thing to go."

"But it's leather and it's beautiful," said Ryan.

"Do you want it?"

"It doesn't really go with the pool house decor. I wish I could take it, though."

"I'll bet it would be good for your brooding sessions." Julie laughed. "Joke, okay?"

Ryan just held out a hand to help Julie up from the couch and over some toppled boxes.

She shrugged and went back to poking in a box.

Ryan kept moving things, but his mind was wandering. He felt proud for getting out of Chino and at the same time he felt ashamed that he hadn't done it all by himself. He hated the fact that he needed so much help now in life. As soon as he had opened the door to caring about people, he seemed to need them even more. He missed feeling self-reliant: He knew self-reliant had meant being lonely but there were times he wondered how he would get along in life without the Cohens.

And he suddenly realized, no one knew that for all the money she had, there was one thing Julie Cooper was missing in her life: a good friend.

Ryan spent most of the morning stacking and moving boxes, leaving just enough space between them so Julie could maneuver around and sort through what was junk or salvageable. They actually had had a few good laughs trying to get several of the chairs, sofas, and lamps out of the unit for disposal. At one point Ryan even found himself worrying that it was too much physical labor for her.

"Maybe we should get someone to help us, like a moving company?" he suggested as they struggled with the leather sofa.

"There isn't anyone," Julie said shortly, not bothering to explain. Ryan wondered if she didn't want to spend the money to hire someone or if she couldn't.

Julie shook her head. "I just want my new place done by the new year so I have someplace to call my own. You know what I mean?" she asked earnestly.

"Sort of, I guess." Julie was confusing Ryan. He wondered if the best thing to do wasn't just to nod and keep working.

Julie opened the back of her SUV so they could start loading stuff into it. She switched on the radio as they began. Suddenly the announcer's voice faded into commercials. Both Ryan and Julie stared at each other when they heard the sharp tweak and squeal of Summer's high-pitched voice over the radio.

"*Help us help others. Join in the fun and give up your Barbies to support the New Playgrounds for Needy Neighbors fundraiser. We at the National Charity League are in need of your old Barbie dolls and accessories in order to make playgrounds in our surrounding areas safe, sound, and okay for kids to hit the ground running. Thank you and once again: Think fun, think ahead, and think playgrounds without lead."*

This was followed by details on how to donate the dolls.

"Wow, that was pretty good. I guess we know what Summer's been up to with Kirsten." Ryan laughed.

"Hey, I know I have a ton of Barbies in one of those boxes. Really old ones, too." She looked at Ryan. "Not *that* old. I'm talking some of mine and some of Marissa's."

"Should you ask Marissa first if she wants to get rid of them?"

"She hasn't played with her Barbies since she learned about boys in first grade. I mean, it's not like I am taking away her Care Bear."

"What is in all those boxes anyway?"

"A lot of stuff I don't need anymore. Plates and glasses, linens and comforters, and — oh, I could probably fill a dozen apartments."

"Well, why don't you?" asked Ryan.

"What do you mean?"

"Instead of just throwing it out, let's give it away."

"I was going to give it to Goodwill," she said defensively.

"I didn't mean it like that. I meant that with your style, all that stuff, and furniture and boxes filled with nice secondhand sheets and towels, and my ability to hang a few shelves pretty quickly, I'll bet we could change a few houses into places kids want to go home to."

"You mean like in the old neighborhood?" She shook her head. "I can't go back there, Ryan. I just can't."

"Well, we could go to Chino. I know a

lot of people in Chino who would never be able to afford a leather couch and we just took two of them out of the storage room."

"There are three chairs behind those big boxes."

"Wow. I'll even bet that pool table leaning against the back wall could go to some rec hall." Ryan raised his eyebrows, hoping to get through to Julie.

"Well, I really wanted to get this project done," she sighed.

"What if I gave you a few days after Chrismukkah, too?"

Julie looked at Ryan with surprise, then smiled and clapped her hands together.

"We could be like *Extreme Makeover*. We'll pick a house a day and just do the best we can until the end. We can use all that stuff in boxes and I know I can get more from people — well, at least those people who are still speaking to me. I'll make some phone calls and get us a truck."

Julie pounded her fists on the table like a drumroll. "This is going to be great — but there is one rule."

"What is that?" asked Ryan.

"We do not cross the line into Riverside. Okay?"

"Okay."

Julie Cooper held out her hand and Ryan took it. They shook for a moment and as he let go he realized that Julie had something he never thought was possible: a heart.

This was the fourth night in a row Seth had been alone to light the candles at Chrismukkah. He wondered exactly where his plan had gone right and wrong. Although he was amazed at how well everyone had embraced their jobs and the fervor with which they seemed to throw themselves into the projects they were assigned, he couldn't believe that after all of his genius and amazing special Seth Sauce added to the events, he was alone again.

Jimmy Cooper had called four days ago to say he would be delayed, and he wanted Seth to go out and prove himself in small ways.

"Come on, Seth — don't you know the slogan 'Think Globally, Act Locally.'"

"Uh, well, the few times I've seen that bumper sticker, it was on a car that I thought should be headed for a California emissions test and it usually had other bumper stickers like 'Hang Up and Drive,' 'Fur Is Bad Karma,' and 'A Lottery Is a Tax on the People.' So I am not exactly sure what you mean."

"Seth, since I've been out here I've realized what damage we do to our environment. Right now I am part of a private boating and yacht club that patrols the waters at night to report people fishing illegally. It's a problem that has only escalated with the popularity of sushi bars across the United States. Because of the seasonal tide shifts there's a range of currents that are bringing dolphins, for example, closer in to the shore so we need to be extra careful to patrol and cut any nets the illegal fishermen drop into the sea."

"That sounds like quite a pirate operation." Seth sighed.

"Well, I wish you could be here, Seth. I know how much you love sailing. The waters are so incredible at night. I know you would be a real asset to our team. If I'd known we were going to be partners I would have made arrangements to have you here. We could use your skills," said Jimmy.

Seth sat up straighter and felt proud. So few people really appreciated his skills as a sailor — sure, he'd had a few bumps and eventually relied on Greyhound to get him out of some tough moments, but overall he was a man who could manage the waters. He, too, wished he were sailing next to Jimmy under the stars, searching for illegal fishermen like some vigilante group from Waterworld.

"Since you can't be here, Seth, I thought you could just go out every day and try to do small things for people: help them carry their groceries to the car, stand on a street corner and look for older people who need help, or just see who is out there and practice extra kindness. I mean, that is also part of the Christmas Hanukkah season, right?"

"Sure. I'll do that if you promise we can spend a serious day on the water sailing together before the new year."

"Absolutely! I want reports, though, Seth. I mean, I probably can't compete with Kirsten or Julie on donations to your favorite charity but at least I want to know you're trying."

Seth looked at the four candles that burned on the menorah. He thought that the miracle of Hanukkah was that there had only been enough oil to last one night and for some reason it lasted eight days, just long enough for the Jewish people to purify the other oil and be able to use it. The miracle of Christmas, he thought, was that a simple child born to simple parents would sacrifice himself for others. Over the past four days he felt he had done neither anything miraculous nor for humanity. It wasn't that he hadn't tried. Oh, he had tried, but what had shocked him was how awful people had been when he did try.

On the first day he thought he was off to a good start. He waited on the corner of Blue Lantern and Santa Clara, not too far from the marina, hoping to be helpful. He figured since everyone was shopping for Christmas, and their arms were overloaded with packages, assisting them to their cars would be easy.

He had approached a middle-aged woman who seemed out of breath as she pushed the electronic door opener to her Cadillac SUV.

"Ma'am may I help you with your bags?"

"Help me what?"

"Well, I thought I could place them in your trunk."

"Back off. If I wanted to tip the valet I would have had him follow me out like an overgrown puppy."

Seth was surprised but persistent. "No, miss, I am just trying to be helpful for the holiday season and wanted to provide you with an extra set of arms. You look weighed down."

"Whom are you working for?"

"No one. I'm really just trying to be helpful."

"Well, you are really just being annoying. Do you know how many people hit you up at Christmastime for tips and donations? It's an endless parade of open palms all waiting for some cash!"

Seth was so surprised he started to back away.

"That's right. Be ashamed of yourself

for trying to take money away from some real charity by hustling me for a few bucks. Carry my bags to the car? What the hell do they have valets for anyway?"

Seth got on his skateboard and tried to make sense of why the woman had screamed at him. Was it true? Did people really expect bigger tips during the holidays? Were donations harder to come by? Was it a competition for money or to prove who had the most needy cause?

Seth thought about his mother and how she was always involved in raising money for some charity or making donations herself. Was it annoying to other people? He had never thought about the people who really needed charity. What if you really relied on times when people felt more generous in order to take care of your family? He knew that during the days before Christmas his parents made a stack of envelopes they kept by the door for all the people who delivered things, worked in the garden, and cleaned house. Sandy had said that the Christmas bonus was an important part of the year and tipping wasn't necessary but it was always appreciated. It shocked him that the woman was so angry about being forced to tip him when he was really just trying to help. In his own way, Seth became even more resolved to help people without asking for anything in return.

On the second day that he had gone out to help people he thought he would do better in the supermarket. He walked up and down the aisles helping people reach for things or load large cumbersome bags of dog food into their carts. He began to notice a man in a suit following him from aisle to aisle.

"Excuse me, son, but what exactly are you doing?"

Seth refrained from his usual answer.

Although he wanted to look the stern-faced red-cheeked security guard in the eye and be sarcastic, he simply shrugged and said, "I'm just trying to be helpful."

"Well, son, we hire people to do that. If you want to apply for a job you can take an application at the courtesy desk."

"But I don't want a job. I just want to be helpful."

"Well, it's a legal problem to have you just helping people without being under the insurance umbrella of our staff accident policy."

"What? My dad's a lawyer. I can't imagine someone would sue just because I helped them."

The security guard let out a hard laugh. "Son, you don't know a thing about California, do you? Where are you from?"

"I'm from here," Seth said defensively.

"Well, then, you better call your lawyer

daddy and ask him some questions, but right now you must leave the store before I have to call in the authorities."

"I'm just trying to help!" Seth pleaded.

"Well, go do it on your own property because we are not taking legal responsibility for your voluntary actions that could lead to any number of accidents."

"What? You think I'm going to spill dog food on someone and they're going to sue me?"

"No, son — not you. They'll sue the store, or the chain of stores, for having an untrained, unauthorized volunteer assist them with their packages or purchases."

"I've never heard of such insanity!" cried Seth as he was gently pushed out of the store.

"Welcome to the OC," snarled the security guard and gave him one final shove through the glass doors.

Seth had been so frustrated he had called Jimmy. But like Marissa often complained, all he got was his voice mail.

He was really looking forward to talking to everyone about their days and was shocked when Marissa called in to say she and Sandy would be staying late to finish shredding some files and cleaning up the office. Then Summer called in to say she and Kirsten were being interviewed by a radio station during rush hour to get more support for New Playgrounds for Needy Neighbors. And Ryan? He thought for sure Ryan would be there to help him settle the score at PlayStation, but even Ryan had called to say he was sorry but he and Julie were taking a drive down to Chino.

Seth looked at the large cardboard chart he had made for the adults to vote on everyone's performance. He began to draw in large red bars for Summer's performance.

It was obvious by the way Summer was so excited over the phone that she and Kirsten were doing a great job collecting Barbies, generating more support, and selling an insane number of tickets to the Barbie auction. Seth was so confused. He thought Barbie was the all-out babe enemy. Every girl was always bitching that Barbie was so perfect that no one could live up to her as a role model. Summer had disagreed with him fiercely.

"Seth — it is not like that at all. Barbie has made a huge transition in our society. Although she does represent some aspects of traditional oppression, no, subjugation, tyranny — no, too strong — well, possible inability to manifest high body standards . . . whatever. On the other hand, Barbie has now moved through fifty years of evolution into the women's movement and has taken her original concept from homemaker into sports, fashion, driving, and even a large business wardrobe, which proves she's a better reflection of the evolution of feminism than Camille Paglia or Naomi Wolf could ever really argue with. Okay, Seth — must go now. Time to tape our spot."

That was Summer? *His Summer?* Silly, superficial, fashion fascist, high-heel honor code, hair product deluxe, perfume perfection, and not too brainy. A few days with his mother and Summer was starting to sound like a woman who wore patchouli oil and debated the value of women in the military while driving a VW bus.

Obviously Summer was earning her stripes.

Marissa was also strange when she called.

"Hey, Seth. Listen, I really know you want us to light those candles and talk about the value of the miracles or something, but your dad said he will totally explain. We have some major research to do over at the Berkeley Law Library. There are some cases I just can't access online that are specific to supporting the defense of the beach vendors under the arts sanction."

"Uh-huh?" asked Seth.

"You know. That case your dad is working on about trying to get real artists to sell their crafts, jewelry, scarves, and nice handmade pieces on the boardwalk without having to apply for the really expensive vendors' license. We're looking through the codes that once altered the license approval during the early 1970s. I think it's really cool. It would bring such a nice aspect of local culture and boutique shopping to the strip, don't you think?"

"Yeah, I guess." But Seth couldn't guess. He didn't know what his father was working on and it confounded him that Marissa seemed so wrapped up and actually in charge of what she was doing. Marissa, who so often wavered and could barely decide what dress to wear to her next function, sounded as if she was learning something invaluable about herself and at the same time gaining a passion for finding inroads for artists to sell their work. Yes — Seth thought, it would be cool if there were real artists selling their crafts along the boardwalk. It would add a lot to the atmosphere even if it would make skating a lot more crowded and difficult.

He colored in a few bars more for Marissa since she seemed to be defending a noble cause.

When Ryan called, Seth was sure he was losing his mind.

"Hey, Seth — sorry, Julie and I can't make it for those candles you want to light."

"I'm sorry, Ryan, did you just mention you and Julie in the same sentence?"

"Well, uh, yeah, I guess I did."

"Okay, I am seriously wondering what drug everyone took to make you all so damn happy helping each other out that you don't have time to come home and complain."

"Seth? Are you losing it?"

"No, dude, you are all obviously losing it. I am the only one sane enough to see that the world does not want help! The world is perfectly happy being miserable and suing each one another for dropping dog food on their toes!"

"Let me guess. I'm not the only one skipping out on dinner?" Ryan asked.

"Bingo-bango-bongo, I don't want to leave the jungle. *No one* is coming home! This is the fourth day in a row everyone is so busy being helpful."

"Seth. Take a deep breath. I thought you would be proud. After all, you were the one who wanted us to learn the true meaning of Chrismukkah and assigned us to be Santa's little helpers."

"Yeah, yeah, you're totally right but what I didn't expect was that Summer would uncover her true feminist self through redecorating Barbie's Minivan, that Marissa could turn out to be an advocate for the arts on the boardwalk, and that you, Ryan Atwood, would be driving a truck around Chino with Julie Cooper wearing a tool belt, playing happy homemaker!"

"Seth, we're not playing house — we are really helping people feel good about their spaces. We bought this totally cool book on feng shui and we're trying to help people figure out what their natural elements are," defended Ryan.

Julie Cooper chimed in from the background: "And color! Oh, we are doing so much to get rid of the blahs in those little ghettos — oh, sorry, Ryan."

"Can you guys hear yourself? Do you think you should have your own television show or what?"

"Listen, Seth — I just called to say we wouldn't be home until later and by that time I'm going to be exhausted and all I'll want to do is get this plaster out of my hair and crawl into bed."

"Well, all *I* want is to be helpful without someone escorting me off the premises or accusing me of stealing tips from Santa Claus."

"Seth? How much coffee have you had?" Ryan asked.

"Not enough."

"Well, it sounds like plenty, if you ask me. Maybe you should just cuddle up on the couch and watch a good movie or something. Hey, you can come out and help us tomorrow if Jimmy isn't back yet."

"Oh, yeah, like what I really want is to watch Julie use a hammer in her Manolo Blahniks and help you move furniture."

"You'd be amazed how rewarding it is, Seth. People are so happy to see their world change right before their eyes. If anyone had done it at our house, I might have felt different about coming home — even when my mother was looped."

Seth let out an exasperated sigh and flopped onto the couch. Leave it to Ryan to always bring home the solid reality check. He loved him as a brother, but sometimes he hated how much Ryan knew about the real world. It was always Ryan who managed to show Seth that there was another side of the story and a darker side of the fence.

"I'll see you over coffee in the morning," said Seth.

"Hold on. Hey, what time did we

promise to get into that house on Mountain Avenue?"

"We're only dropping off that couch before they go to work, and then we need to get right over to Central and make sure those guys we hired finished painting last night so we can hang the new drapes."

"I'll have to see about coffee, Seth. I think we might just hit the road early. We need to get into some house before people go to work."

"Oh my god! Man, can you hear yourself? The next thing you're going to tell me is that Julie Cooper has Carhartt pants and Timberland boots on."

Seth could hear Julie laughing as Ryan repeated his comment.

"But they *are* pink," said Ryan.

"Hello — Earth to Ryan!" screamed Seth in exasperation. "You are sitting next to the Wicked Witch of the West — even worse, she is the vixen of the OC. Has your brain been vaporized by the soul-stealing nymph?"

"I think she's too old to be a nymph, Seth."

"I can't take it, Ryan. This is more disgusting than catching her lip-smacking Luke at the Mermaid."

"Don't go there, Seth. It isn't very nice at this time of year. Aren't there things that should be forgiven and forgotten?"

"This is Christmas, not a pardon on death row!"

"Bye, Seth. I hope Jimmy comes home soon. You need some guidance."

Seth flipped his phone closed and threw it across the room. What he felt like he really needed was a good dose of the mall. If no one was showing up to be his guiding mentor maybe it was a sign from the great gods of Chrismukkah that he didn't need a mentor and he was really already engulfed in the spirit of giving. All of these great things were happening because of him, weren't they? He really didn't need one. He was probably just too mature and knew where his talents were. If Jimmy was busy saving dolphins, Marissa and Sandy were supporting the arts, Summer and Kirsten were playing with Barbies, and Ryan and Julie were wrecking homes (which seemed only too appropriate), then maybe it was up to him to test the new PlayStation and decide if it was suitable for kids. He could always say he did some technical research to protect America's youth from unnecessary violence. After all, there was an incredible amount of blood and gore in certain video games and parents should be forewarned before buying inappropriate material. Seth could definitely save some virginal eyes and ears by doing the research at the mall and then reporting it at parent Web sites and other blogs that supported parent blocks and screening. He settled into the couch and began to make a list of all the games he would preview tomorrow at the mall.

THE

7

The mall was awash in the glitter and tinsel that Seth had begun to miss. Hanging around his house empty of its usual mammoth tree decorated in white, the menorahs on the mantles, and festive decorations throughout the rooms, he felt he'd started some strange chain reaction by making everyone work so hard for their gifts. At home, Chrismukkah now barely registered except in the labored days of hustling projects to raise money or give it away.

Deep in the mall canyons and three-story waterfalls, there were bright green-and-red balls hanging from the ceiling, and flashing lights outlined words like *Joy, Season's*

Greetings, Happy Holidays. Santa's reindeer were sailing through the air over the escalators with their legs kicking joyously, and Rudolph's nose illuminated the glass dome like a lighthouse beacon on a dark night.

Seth ordered his third mochaccino and ran back and forth to electronics stores trying out new versions of the portable PlayStation. The pure manic indulgence of it kept him from thinking about the fact that in reality he wasn't doing anything for anyone but himself. He tried to take notes in his head regarding the games but it was a useless exercise. He would start by critiquing one and then get wrapped up either playing it or competing with another kid for points. He would allow his mind to focus entirely on winning and not at all on educating anyone on the Internet.

Once during a heated battle as he scaled the wall and fought off the master, and two other kids just entering puberty, he realized how badly he had to go to the bathroom. All those mochaccinos had him cranked but he was getting starry-eyed and very uncomfortable. Finally he had to relinquish his controller and run through the crowded mall to the men's room.

Seth was sure this, too, was like some wild ride and could, or should, definitely be a PlayStation game. Running to the bathroom, hurdling over small kids and sunglasses stands, and squeezing through display sale racks was a talent only a true ninja master of the twenty-first century could manage. He was the Ironist, the man of the hour, flying, soaring, moving with speed and grace until he pushed open the bathroom door as if knocking down a castle wall or dungeon barricade and saw Santa Claus lying on the floor.

For a moment Seth thought he really was in the middle of his own video game.

He was sure he had slipped into another dimension and was now speeding through his memory bank about to decipher if Santa was a spy. Of course, he also knew he shouldn't drink so much caffeine because it had a strange effect on his nervous system and imagination. He splashed some water on his face and bent down to check if Santa was breathing.

"Hey, buddy, uh, Santa, are you okay?"

Seth knew it wasn't right to shake a victim if you were unclear as to what had happened. There was a small puddle of water near Santa's beard but other than that there were no traces of foul play. Seth shook his head again. He had to stop thinking like one of his own cartoon characters. He took a deep breath and poked Santa on the shoulder.

Santa groaned a little and coughed but did not seem particularly coherent. Seth could not believe how badly he had to pee. Why was it that when he was faced with a severe situation, like saving a life, his body usually had other plans. He ran back through the doors and tried to get help in the closest department store.

"Hey, Santa passed out — can you call a medic or security?" he screamed at the lady behind the perfume counter. Why was it that perfume was always the first thing you had to deal with at a department store? Why were the perfume counters always like some wave of floral insanity you had to get through to buy a tie?

"Uh, lady, did you hear me?"

"It's not my department."

"We are talking about someone's life here, not paying for a handbag."

The young woman barely moved.

"*Hello*! Can you pick up that phone and dial for some help?" Seth had had enough of people not being helpful. He was down-right tired of everyone being so concerned with themselves that Santa Claus might be dying and the store clerk didn't care.

Seth reached over the glass counter and pulled on the phone.

The girl shrieked. "Help! Help! It's a robbery!"

Seth looked at her with shocked and amazed eyes.

"No, no, no, I told you — Santa is sick in the bathroom."

She looked at him and screamed, "Sick kid! Did you mug Santa? Help! Security! Thief!"

Seth realized that two security cameras had turned on him and three security guards were running down the aisles toward the counter. Faced with the need for an instant decision, he decided it was best, since of course he still had to pee, to lead them directly back to Santa. He had the slim hope of going to the bathroom before he had to call his father to come bail him out.

Seth was particularly glad he had just practiced maneuvering through the mall at such high speed and grace because he certainly needed it now. He threw the phone back at the girl, who was so startled she picked up a testing bottle of perfume and began to spray it at him like mace. As he slipped away, Seth saw she had nailed one of the security guards in the face, bringing them all to a halt.

Seth stopped and dropped his arms to his side in a huff. *Oh, for crying out loud!* he thought. *I'm the only person I know who is being chased in hot pursuit and needs to wave his arms like a windmill for them to follow.* Seth stuck his fingers between his teeth and let out a piercing whistle. It was something his grandmother had taught him about hailing a taxi in New

York. He was ridiculously proud of his ability to do it and rarely got the chance. This was the perfect opportunity. The whistle echoed off the marble walls of the mall and also managed to gain the attention of several other shoppers and more officious-looking security men now running through the atrium toward him.

Bingo — I'm out of here. Seth began his laborious run through the hall, circling back down toward the bathrooms. The security guards were close enough behind that he could hear them shouting, "He's heading for the bathroom!"

When he entered, Santa had moved from the floor and was now propped up along the wall by the urinal. Seth thought for sure something must be wrong with this man since no one in his right mind would sit so close to that very spot. At least he was breathing and it gave Seth just enough time to slip into a stall.

He heard the swinging doors to the bathroom slam against the wall.

"Come out here with your hands up."

Seth walked slowly out of the stall with his hands high in the air.

"Place your hands on top of your head."

"But I haven't washed them."

"Don't be smart, young man, put them on top of your head."

Seth started to bring his hands down to his sides.

One of the security guards pulled out a gun and held it so nervously that Seth had to do everything to fight back a laugh.

"Listen, I didn't do anything. I was trying to get that girl to call you guys because of Santa here."

"You can tell it to the chief of security."

"Okay, okay, but would you just look at Santa? Who in his right mind would choose that spot to make themselves comfortable?"

Seth felt sure they would suddenly see his point.

Instead, however, the older guard sighed and put his hand on his hip.

"You mean to tell us you created a huge scene, disturbed the peace, assaulted a store clerk, all in the name of saving Buckeye?"

"Buck who?" asked Seth.

The guard who had been holding the gun let it slowly drop back into his holster, which he missed three times. "Darn. . . . Did you by chance ask Buckeye if he was all right?"

"Yes, but he was barely breathing," said Seth defensively.

"Barely breathing, huh? Well, he looks fine to me." They began to slowly gather themselves and move toward Seth.

Seth took a step back. "Wait a minute, wait a minute here, I don't get it. You look like you are about to arrest me."

"Well, Buckeye might be drunk but you are disorderly in public."

"Santa is drunk?"

"Well, he looks like he has passed through drunk now and is much closer to passed out. Come on, kid, let's get the questioning over with at the main hub."

"What about Santa? Who's going to take Santa in?"

"Well, I guess they'll fire him again and get a replacement but at this time of year it isn't easy. This is a nonequity job so all the extras can't take it, and since most people are already booked I have no idea what personnel is going to do."

"We are talking about a drunk guy having kids sit on his lap and tell them all their wishes," said Seth.

"Son. This is Newport. There are more kids with credit cards in their pockets than lost wishes on Santa."

"Now come with us or we'll have to cuff you."

Seth held his hands out to be cuffed and the older security guard smiled.

"Wash them first."

As Seth sat through routine questioning, he was completely disturbed that they might allow a drunken Santa to head back out onto the floor. Either all those kids waiting in line wouldn't get to whisper their secret wishes or, worse yet, when they did, Santa would belch beer in their faces.

"Hey, kiddo, can you answer the question?"

"I'm sorry. I was thinking about that guy . . . Buckeye."

"Yes, he is kind of a sad case," said Officer Crumb, the head of security.

"What do you mean?"

"Well, he was once a famous Santa Claus. He starred in all the old Hollywood classics. He was the best Santa there ever was. Kids just loved him and he never went anywhere without people whispering in his ear for special things. As if he could make miracles."

"And then what? I mean what happened? He doesn't look that old."

"Well, I guess he started to feel like he couldn't save everyone. The more people mistook him for Santa, the more they actually confided in him."

"Life took a hard turn for him once when a kid asked if he could save his mother from some kind of jail sentence."

"But that's not realistic," defended Seth.

"Well, tell it to the kid. The next year Buckeye was suiting up, happy every year at this time to be everyone's secret-keeper, and that kid came back. Oh, man, it makes what you did in the mall look like a bad video game."

Seth was insulted but he wanted to know the end of the story.

"Well, the kid was so shook up that his mother had been sent back to prison that he attacked Santa and started screaming he was a fake and a loser and that he could never help people and he had trusted him and Santa couldn't make miracles. From then on Buckeye lost his focus. He stopped laughing altogether and never smiled anymore for pictures, and well, it was just a matter of time before he turned to the bottle."

Seth tipped back in the hard plastic chair. "That is a really sad story," said Seth.

"Sure is, kid. Now the mall just keeps him on payroll but he's pretty much worthless. I guess this year they'll have to let him go. This is the worst it has ever been."

"I wish there was someone to help him," said Seth, wondering how hard it must be to be in charge of so many dreams and never be able to make any of them come true.

"Oh, a lot of people have tried but he's just given up. When he gets really drunk he just walks around mumbling that kid's name over and over."

"How many years ago was that?" asked Seth.

"Over ten years. I remember because my own son is about the same age. So I guess that kid must have been five or six at the time. That's a tough way to find out Santa doesn't exist."

"Who is going to be Santa for the rest of the day?" asked Seth.

"Oh, I don't know. We'll find someone. Poor kids."

Just then a long-legged blond girl came through the security doors dressed in a very short green velvet skirt with white trim and big red buttons down her bolero jacket. She had on bright red lipstick and an elf hat.

"Mr. Crumb, the kids are all getting really crazy in line. If I hand out any more lollipops they'll go into a sugar coma and we'll be peeling them off the ceiling. Isn't there anyone who can be Santa for the rest of the day?"

Seth took one look at Santa's little helper and volunteered for the job.

Officer Crumb laughed so hard he fell off his chair and spilled his large bucket of paper clips onto the floor.

"What? I'm a flexible guy. I'm on school break. I would hate to see all those kids disappointed."

The pretty girl smiled.

"That is mighty grand of you, kid, but first I have to press some charges here. Second of all, I hate to say it, but you're a little too young, a little too thin, and well, you just don't look the part."

"Are you saying I can't be Santa because I'm Jewish? Isn't that discrimination? Isn't that against the law? Doesn't everyone have a right to the same job whether they are man, woman, Caucasian, African-American, Asian, Indian, or Jewish?" Seth stood up and knew he had him on a very small technicality.

"Well, it's not up to me but I'll let personnel know you're interested in the job," chuckled Crumb.

"Just give me a chance. I know I can do it. I know I can. Why don't we make a trade? I'll finish off the day as Santa and we'll call it my community service for disorderly conduct in the mall?"

"You're pretty funny, kid. What do you want to be when you grow up — a lawyer?"

"Definitely not."

"Okay. There're only a few hours left in the day anyway. I'll call up to personnel and let them know what happened and see if we can dig you up some extra padding and a beard from the costume store. Clarisse? Would you show our new Santa behind the velvet ropes and into the locker room?"

"Sure, Mr. Crumb, but how are we going to get the suit off of Buckeye?"

"Oh, he's down in the infirmary. I'll take care of that and meet you outside the men's changing locker."

Seth followed Clarisse through the catacombs behind the mall stores and knew that if Summer found him standing so close to this beautiful blond elf with a sweet smile and even sweeter legs he would certainly find himself with a nose like Rudolph.

THE OC

8

Seth was up early although he knew everyone else in the house was sleeping. He wanted to draw a few sketches of Clarisse. It was now the sixth day of Hanukkah and there hadn't been one night that the crew had come together to light the menorah, discuss the prayers and miracles, or practice making gingerbread cake. The large cardboard diagram with all of their names on it and how well they were doing earnestly helping others had been filled in with several different colored markers.

It amazed Seth that someone had remembered to mark their progress when he wasn't there. It looked like Julie had taken some extra time to rate Ryan as spectacular and she drew all sorts of exclamation points and stars around his score. It was sickening to Seth. Kirsten had rated Summer with small Barbie stickers on top of her perfectly drawn tower of bold red marker, and Sandy had sketched in some waves around Marissa's report. From what Seth could see, they were all running a competitive game to be perfect except for him. Jimmy Cooper was still deep in the waves and no one had filled in Seth's chart. He actually shrugged it off, a strange moment for Seth, who usually suffered from severe obsessive disorders and competition. He realized that the kids had really made him laugh yesterday as they sat on his lap with their long lists and sudden apologies for pushing Marcie Cunningham's hair into the pencil sharpener, or dressing the cat up like Hercules.

Seth realized he was up early because

he actually looked forward to going to the mall today. He had done such an enthusiastic job as Santa that even when one of the kids pulled off his fake beard he managed to convince him Santa was really busy trying to figure out how to master the seventh level of the new PlayStation before he put it under the tree. Personnel said he was definitely wrong for the part, but a few goose-down pillows made up for most of it, and besides, with only a few days left to go there was no one else around. Seth knew his special brand of humor made him endearing to everyone who worked around him, especially Clarisse.

Clarisse was from a local public school and knew nothing about Seth's world of high school dramas. She knew no Anna, no Summer, and especially no Zach. Zach had really worn on his nerves throughout the year. It always seemed like he was in the shadows waiting for something to go wrong between Summer and Seth — and since that happened often enough, Clarisse provided Seth with a fresh look at life.

Clarisse had taken on the job of Santa's little helper to make extra money to buy her family gifts for Christmas. It was her task to make sure the kids stayed in line and keep them from pushing too hard or stepping on one another's toes by waving a finger and saying: "He knows if you've been good. . . ." Or "He's watching you right now."

Clarisse also helped hand out lollipops and made sure parents understood where to pick up their child's Santa picture at the photo concession stand. Seth Cohen realized his smile was always a little bigger when Clarisse was watching.

He began to sketch her long legs and cute tummy with the glitter belly ring that stuck out from under her bolero elf jacket. He was deep into her muscular stomach and curves when he felt a slap on the back.

"Hey, Seth, it's been a while. Good morning," said his father.

Seth placed a protective arm around his sketchbook.

"Something new in the works?" asked Sandy. "I thought you gave that up for a while after, well, you know, Little Miss Vixen was so angry."

"I guess it is just the holiday spirit. I need to release a little pent-up energy."

Sandy Cohen was good at defending you but he was lousy at boundaries. He leaned right over Seth and stared at the sketch of Clarisse's lower body.

"Hey, that is cute. Now I'd be all for celebrating Christmas if Santa's helpers looked like that. Do you want a bagel?"

"No, Dad, I'm good."

"So how have you been spending your days, Seth? Things have been so busy at the office. I can't believe what a help Marissa is. She has really grounded herself in the material and shows real promise of a good defensive legal brain."

"Well, years of lying to Julie Cooper must have taught her how to defend herself," sighed Seth. He stood up and closed his sketchbook.

"Oh, yeah — have you spoken to Ryan?" Sandy asked.

The door to the kitchen opened and Ryan stepped in.

"Speak of the devil," said Sandy. "And like I said — speaking of devils . . . how are you surviving your renovating projects with Julie?"

Ryan rubbed his eyes and stared at Sandy and Seth, then he shrugged, stretched, and nodded.

Sandy looked surprised. "So it's not that bad, huh?"

Ryan reached for a cup of coffee. "It's really okay."

"Whoa, whoa, whoa, I didn't even hear a response to the first question. Dad, how did you get all that from him taking a deep breath?"

"I pick juries, Seth. I gotta know body language."

"Well, I wish I could do that. He summed up six days of work with a shrug and a yawn."

"Speaking of speaking, or whatever we are doing, what are you doing with your time?" asked Ryan.

Seth froze. He hadn't actually thought about what he was going to tell people when they asked what he was doing. Besides, he was really afraid that if they found out they would come visit him and worse yet, blow his cool cover with Clarisse.

"Well, I'm spending my days helping people."

"Great. Helping them what?" asked Kirsten, entering the room.

Seth knew he wanted to say something but instead of taking Ryan's cool stance and leaning against the counter he began to wave his hands in the air and sputter short syllables and sounds until he was sure he had said something that made no sense at all because Kirsten, Ryan, and Sandy stared at him and nodded slowly in disbelief.

"Sounds like you're having some adventures, honey." Kirsten patted him on the head. "Hey, I think Summer and I will be late again tonight. We just got a shipment of forty dolls from a warehouse in Burbank. This is the last round we have to make over before setting them up for the auction and charity ball. So I am really sorry, Seth honey, but I do not think we'll make the candle lighting."

"That's okay, Mom," Seth said, suddenly remembering that the mall was open late. He would be staying until nine P.M. and if he was lucky, he could take a walk with Clarisse after work. If anyone did want to come to the candle lighting he was in trouble.

"What about you, Dad?" asked Seth.

"Well, in all honesty, Seth, Marissa has been working so hard I wanted to take her for a trial surf after work. The tide is just perfect for her to get comfortable in, some light white water, and she said she would try it. If we could beg off I promise to be here tomorrow night."

"Why don't we all do that?" said Seth.

Ryan squinted at him from one eye.

"Tomorrow night is the last night before the charity ball anyway. It is the seventh

149

day of Project Chrismukkah and I think we'll be able to tell who is going to be voted Most Valuable Player," continued Seth.

"Sounds good to me. Marissa is without a doubt a lifesaver on this case." Sandy smiled. "She is so good at describing the law in simple terms to the artisans, I am really impressed."

"Oh, don't count Summer out. She has proven herself to be worth her weight in gold. I honestly don't know what I would have done without her. Not only is she talented at repainting and refurbishing the dolls, she keeps me laughing when things get serious," challenged Kirsten.

Seth thought of how often Summer helped him out of his mental funks and depressions with one of her observations on the superficial things in life. He did smile to himself.

Ryan yawned. "Sounds good to me. I know that means Julie and I can finish a few houses when people come home from work."

"What do you mean, Ryan?" Kirsten looked confused. It was obvious they had all been working so hard they had missed one another.

"Well, if we had lit the candles and met to discuss minor miracles, then you would know the biggest miracle of them all is that Julie Cooper and I are becoming best friends." Ryan replied with a grimace that made Seth laugh so hard he knocked over the bagels.

"What?" asked Sandy. "I thought you were helping her move some stuff into her new place now that she — well, you know . . ." Sandy raised an eyebrow in Kirsten's direction. Things had not gone well during the Caleb fiasco and many people still had their doubts about Julie's involvement.

Ryan shrugged.

"NO! NO! NO! No shrugging! I want words, man! Give us some words!" Seth yelled.

"Cool out. We actually thought our time would be better spent doing quick renovations on houses around Chino."

"What the heck?" said Sandy.

"She had so much furniture and stuff like curtains and sheets and things left over from all the times she redecorated that I said we could really make a difference if we didn't just throw it away but we gave it away."

"Ryan and Julie are buddies driving around Chino playing *Extreme Makeover*," Seth said in disbelief. "This cannot be happening."

"Seth, you sound kind of jealous," said Kirsten.

"No, just disgusted."

"Everyone has a good and bad side, Seth. It's important to remember that," Kirsten said.

"Actually, Seth, it is a good reminder for today," said Sandy.

"What?"

"Well, every day of Hanukkah has a theme and if today is the sixth day that means we are to take great strides and be ambitious in our appreciation for the miracles around us. If Julie Cooper and Ryan Atwood are playing nice, I'd say that is a major miracle." Sandy slapped Ryan on the back tenderly.

"What impresses me is that you're doing something so genuine for people. How on earth did you get Julie to go back there?" asked Kirsten.

"I promised no Riverside, only Chino. It works. It's nice to see some old friends, and everyone is really happy about what we are adding to their places. It's cool to paint a wall, add some bookshelves, set up the room differently, and watch how happy they are when they come home. I dig it."

"Are you going straight guy with a queer eye on me?" Seth asked.

Ryan punched Seth lightly in the stomach and Seth fell back gasping. "Okay, definitely not. You are still all man, Ryan."

"It looks to me like Ryan might pull off some impressive points, too," said Sandy, kissing Kirsten good-bye.

"Oh, I have to go, too. Summer and I are meeting at this little boutique that's cutting up some of my mom's old Pucci dresses to make culottes. Bye!"

Seth looked up at Ryan. "I know you have to get to your construction crew. Blow outta here."

Ryan held his fist in the air and Seth brought his up to meet it.

"Wonder twins activate," said Seth with a smile and a slight cough.

Ryan waved.

"Next time, big guy, you don't have to punch so hard!"

Seth was happy to be alone again and finish sketching his elfin dream.

Seth waved to Clarisse and she nodded back. Santa's workshop would close for lunch in ten minutes. He had asked Clarisse to eat with him but she had been reluctant at first.

"I totally brown-bag it," she said. "I can't afford the food court."

"Oh, well . . . I was kind of asking you on a date. I mean, not like a date-date because those happen at night, but maybe like a lunch date, a get-to-know-you date, a, well, I just wanted to take you out and since we pretty much work twelve-hour shifts from now until Christmas, a lunch date is about all we can squeeze in." Seth had not meant to use the word *date* at all but he certainly didn't want Clarisse to pay. That was certainly a luxury he could take care of. But the "D" word was dangerous — especially since things with him and Summer were so imbalanced.

"Okay. That sounds great. I know what we'll do. We should get some things to go and then take them to this private spot I know of — very cool." She nodded and winked, causing the bell on the tip of her hat to fall forward and hit Seth in the eye.

"Oh, I'm so sorry," she gasped.

"No, that was great. It was totally something I would have done."

Clarisse closed the velvet ropes and moved the arms on the big clock to show when Santa's Workshop would open up again. She pretended to help Santa out of his chair while he laughed and leaned on her so all the kids thought she was taking him for a nap. When they entered the employee area behind the solid white doors, Seth tore off his beard.

"I get so hot under there. All these pillows in this suit are heavy."

"Yeah, Buckeye used to say he lost ten pounds every Christmas just from sweating in that suit."

"Okay, aside from how gross that makes me feel right about now and wondering if my Arid Extra Dry is holding up, I wonder how long you've known that old guy?"

"Well, I guess since I was a kid, but I didn't really know it. My mother used to work extra shifts here, too, during the holidays and I would just run through the mall. I mean, I hung out a lot with the guys from security and I've basically grown up watching this place expand. But Buckeye was like the grandfather I never had. My family is pretty split up and it's just my mom and me. We would spend Christmas Eve at the mall together and then after the shift we would get together with security and exchange presents and enjoy all the blinking lights and displays in the quiet. Buckeye is a great person. He always made sure we had extra gifts from 'Santa' under the tree.

"Come on, let's change. That life history stuff must be strange and depressing, huh?" she asked.

Seth shook his head. He found Clarisse very authentic and real. She had a quality about her that was similar to Ryan. She was down-to-earth and sincere, somewhat guarded and defensive, but Seth felt like he knew it was because somewhere along the line she had been hurt and disappointed.

Seth bought a bunch of gourmet sandwiches and two large iced mocha coffees and Clarisse led him back into a fire stairwell. He felt like he had been climbing for hours and tried not to look down at the spinning staircase below him. When she opened the door, they were on the roof of the mall on the supportive edge of the glass atrium dome. It felt more like scaffolding than a wall but Clarisse assured Seth she had been out there a thousand times.

It was amazing. You could see all the way into the mountains and back into the mall through the glass with the light blinking below.

"Very cool," said Seth.

Clarisse nodded. "I'm glad you like it. It is just one of those simple things but it always gives me a lift to come out here and know that there's another world before I go back and stand by the rope warning kids not to push one another."

"Well, you won't do it forever," said Seth.

Clarisse looked down. "It feels like I've been here my whole life, and really I have."

Seth put his hand over hers. He knew

this was dangerous territory but he couldn't help himself.

"You seem like a really smart person. I'm sure you'll do other things. What do you like to do?"

"Actually, I'd like to help other people. I always think I have it hard until someone else comes along who has it tougher — and I realize I might not have a lot of money, I might not have a dad I can call, I might not have all the cool things in the mall, but I have a really great extended family here, and my mom works hard and our house is full of love."

As Seth watched the wind blow slightly through Clarisse's hair, she looked much more like an angel than an elf.

"Does that sound way corny?" she asked.

"No, it sounds like you have a pretty good head on your shoulders and a real gift to make others happy."

"Sometimes it seems like money is the only thing that makes people happy," she sighed.

Seth thought of Marissa Cooper. How often she was hurt and how she had all the money in the world now but it certainly hadn't made her happy.

"I know a lot of unhappy people with money," said Seth.

"I just want it so I can give it away to other people. Oh my god!" Her entire face filled with pink warmth and her eyes sparkled with excitement.

"Tomorrow is Kids' Day. It's so wonderful. A bunch of orphans and kids from foster homes are bussed over to the mall and we throw this great party when the mall closes and all the kids just eat themselves sick and open presents and it's the best day out of the whole year! Just to watch them smile and laugh and be carefree is amazing." She had tears in her eyes.

Seth was pretty sure he had never met anyone so genuine before in his life, and right now he knew exactly what his father meant about remaining ambitious to appreciate the miracles around us. And he also realized that he would have to call off the lighting of the candle for just another night. He couldn't disappoint Clarisse and he was also sure he couldn't disappoint all those kids waiting to talk to Santa.

Clarisse sipped her drink.

"Wow. That was a great lunch and this is an awesome coffee."

"I had them load it up with double espresso and two shots of chocolate."

"Thanks for being so sweet." She kissed him on the cheek.

Immediately Seth felt guilty.

"Did I do something wrong?"

"Oh, no. It's just that I have this girl-friend sometimes — and sometimes not. We're really great together when we're great together but a lot of the time we're really awful together." Seth slapped himself on the forehead. "I guess that doesn't make much sense."

Clarisse put her hand on his shoulder. "It makes perfect sense. You seem like the kind of guy that I wouldn't want to let go of even if we were having a few problems." She smiled.

"Thanks. I feel really bad about your friend Buckeye. Think they'll give him his job back?"

"Oh, I'm sure they will. He's like a fixture. He just hits rough patches and then usually pulls himself together. I used to wish that boy would come back and forgive him. I mean, the poor kid was begging Santa not to send his mother away to prison. It was one of the saddest moments I ever remember about being here. My mother was working her extra shifts and I was helping to hand out lollipops and this kid came in on one of the buses and started screaming like crazy. He was so upset. You could see this wild rage and disappointment in his eyes and he was only about six. We were about the same age then so I never forgot it. I always wondered what happened to him, and poor Buckeye obsesses about it even now. I guess in my own way it was how I started to realize there were people who had it a lot worse off than I did."

"You're pretty optimistic for a teenager. Most of us are very busy being angry at our parents and sulking," said Seth.

Clarisse laughed. "Well, I have a secret," she said. "Can I trust you, Santa?"

"Totally."

"Therapy. I've been to therapy and it really helped me." She smiled. "My therapist totally helped me see that I was angry with my mother for making my father leave when really it wasn't her fault at all. If it hadn't been for therapy I might be involved with drugs and some risky behavior."

"Well, you seem pretty adjusted to me."

"Come on, Santa. We better get you dressed again. All those kids are counting on your fluff."

"Clarisse, before we go back to work, do you have any wishes?" Seth asked.

In all of his life Seth had never wanted to help someone so much. He felt she was the most selfless person he had ever met. For all the times he had sulked in his room, he felt ashamed for not making better use of his time by helping others. He felt a surge of love for his dad and realized why it had been so important to him to keep Ryan safe. *I guess it only takes saving one person and you feel like you saved the world.*

"So? Tell me? After all, I am keeping a list," teased Seth.

"It is this silly dream but every year I

work here on Kids' Day I think that kid is going to come walking through the doors and somehow Buckeye will stop drinking and be himself again. I know it is weird, right, because by now that kid is the same age as us — like sixteen or something — but I still see this little boy and his big brown eyes all filled with tears and his matted-down blond hair and I feel like I can just reach out and touch him. I don't know, maybe I remember it all because it was such a turning point in my life. It was when I started to lose the only really good father figure I had ever had in my life."

Seth looked up at the sky and for one moment wished he had been a little more regular about his prayers through life because now he was certainly asking for a miracle. He hoped someone would hear him because for the first time he wasn't asking for himself.

Seth slipped into the kitchen hoping no one would hear him. It was early and he wanted to leave a note saying that he wouldn't make that night's candle lighting and they would all just have to take stock tomorrow night on the eighth day. After all, of the eight days of Hanukkah, that was the day of miracles. He was certainly hoping since everyone was so wrapped up in their own mandates to be helpful that skipping tonight would be a relief. What he worried about most was how he was going to be able to get to his mother's event and still manage to be Santa. At least he had one more day to feign a fever or pretend to get very ill on leftover Thai food. The only person who would probably be angry was Summer. How would he ever explain to Summer that he was playing Santa and couldn't escort her to the ball? The ball that she organized and worked so hard on with his mother. This year things had certainly taken a strange turn.

He had once heard a television personality say that if you want to see how well you are doing in life, go help someone in need. He knew he wasn't doing anything spectacular with his days but he did manage to bring a lot of smiles to some lonely kids and tonight he was really excited to be Santa. He even had a special surprise for Clarisse. He had drained his savings account and made out a bank check in her name so that she could give money away to help some of those people she knew. It was all the money he had made last summer, and he felt really good about just giving it away right now. As he left the bank, he was feeling light-headed with joy and recognized that was actually what the word meant. All the times he had said, "Hey — Joy to you on the holy days, man," he had never really known its true essence. Carrying that check in his wallet for Clarisse to share with needy people made him feel astoundingly proud of himself.

His cell phone rang. He leaped for it in the dark kitchen before anyone heard it.

"Hey, Seth? Is it too early? It's Jimmy."

"Oh, hey. Are you in town yet?"

"Actually, I'm going to be delayed until tomorrow."

"Oh, too bad. I thought you were coming in today," said Seth.

"That was the original plan but we caught a major illegal trolling company fishing after hours last night, and I need to talk to the Coast Guard and our local environmental group."

"Sounds like you are doing your work."

"What about you?"

Seth laughed. "Well, at first it was amazing how hard it was to help people and then I stumbled upon an opportunity that couldn't be missed."

"That was vague, Seth."

"Well, let me just say I have evolved into the mighty corporate leader of Santa's Workshop and I couldn't be happier bringing smiles to hundreds of kids every day."

"Wow. What exactly are you doing?"

Seth worried that he might be overheard and really it sounded too absurd to even say over the phone. He began to make a hissing sound and turned on the fan above the oven.

"Hey, sorry, Jimmy. I can't hear you. I must be losing you."

"Hey . . . wait, Seth. I can't get ahold of Marissa. Every time I leave her a message, the phone is turned off."

"Oh, yes, she is over at the law library a lot and it's one of those serious no-phone zones."

"Will you tell her I'll be there tomorrow?"

"Got it. Can't hear. Got to go. Breaking up." Seth smiled as he put down the phone and tore up his first note. This worked completely to his advantage. He knew Marissa would be depressed and freaked out into one of her eggnog comas that her dad wasn't here yet but it was a great excuse not to have a group lighting of the candles and blame it on Jimmy. On the last night of Hanukkah and the last day of their Santa helpers gifting they would sit down and share their stories and light candles. Seth was certainly hoping to talk Buckeye back into performing as Santa by tomorrow and hoped that he would break down and come see the kids tonight.

Clarisse told him Buckeye never missed a year. No matter what condition he was in, Buckeye couldn't help watching the kids open their gifts and be treated by the mall staff. Seth himself was hoping to get free of his extra weight, pillows and beard, and maybe even spend a few moments in the bouncy house with Clarisse. Seth shook his head. He didn't know what it was about Clarisse that made her so beautiful. Maybe it was just because she had such a good heart.

The light flipped on and Seth jumped.

"Ah!" Seth said.

"Ah!" Marissa said.

"What are you doing here?" Seth asked.

"I slept here last night. I was at the library until midnight and then your dad and I had some late-night takeout. I just crashed on the couch.

"We have a few things to wrap up in the morning and then we are going out for another surf lesson!" Marissa beamed with energy. Seth hadn't seen that fire in her since she first met Ryan.

"You like surfing?" Seth asked.

"Well, it's hard but fun and I've really learned to trust myself on the board. Most of all I think I just enjoy watching your dad get so excited when I can ride the white water all the way in without falling."

Seth was perplexed. "You can do that?"

"Yes. Soon I'm going to be totally Roxy." Marissa laughed. "Is there coffee?"

"Yes. You know where everything is."

Marissa was light on her feet and moved through the kitchen with a bouncy step.

"Hey. Totally weird — I just talked to your dad," said Seth. "If I had known you were here I would have woken you up."

"No problem. He left me some messages but I've spent so much time in the library. They are freaks about that no-phone thing at the law school. I mean, if they even hear you vibrate the librarian gives you a warning." She laughed.

"Well, I got some good news/bad news."

"Is he okay?"

"Yeah. He just busted this big company and they need him to make some statements today so he won't be in until tomorrow." Seth waited for her to break down or start crying.

Marissa opened the refrigerator and said, "Is there any fruit?"

"Did you hear me, Miss Cooper?"

"Yes. Good for my dad. He originally got involved in that environmental stuff because his girlfriend is all into it. But it sounds like he's really committed now. Cool."

Seth picked up Marissa's coffee and smelled it.

"What are you doing?" she asked.

"I'm checking for vodka," he said, sniffing like a rabbit.

"Why?"

"Well, I just told you your dad isn't showing for another day and you want to know if there is fruit. Basically I think you might be drinking or on drugs."

"No, Seth. I'm on a mission. I have a life and a job and a passion."

"A passion?"

"Yes. I think I could be really good at this defending stuff. It is so neat to find all the loopholes and the rules that have been broken. I'm like a total pro at getting out of bad situations — well, of course I need to be coherent — but I get it. I get how to convince people how to look at something differently and then back it up with stories and other cases." She smiled and looked around the room. "There's the fruit."

Marissa Cooper went to work making a large fruit salad and Seth watched her in awe until the door to the pool house opened. Both of their eyes followed Ryan across the patio until he was at the kitchen threshold.

"Good morning," said Marissa.

Ryan looked up and smiled, then looked at Seth and shook his head, then looked back at Marissa as if to recalculate exactly why she was here so early in the morning.

"Catch a ride from your mother?" he asked, looking over Marissa's shoulder for Julie.

"No. I fell asleep on the couch doing some casework for Sandy."

"Oh." Ryan looked hurt.

Marissa shrugged. "I would have come to say hello but your lights were out."

Things had been up in the air again and Seth wasn't sure if they were still pretending not to be in love or pretending to be friends with benefits. He was raptly watching them when Summer's voice echoed in the hall.

"Anyone awake?"

Marissa, Ryan, and Seth all answered, "Kitchen."

"Hi!" Summer bounced into the room, filled with exuberant energy and carrying a large box.

"What's in the box?" asked Marissa.

"Oh my god. These are so amazing. I have ten Barbies from 1950 that I just finished last night. I wanted Kirsten to have them first thing so we can start doing the time line and set up for the ball. Look at them!"

Summer held up a doll in a plastic bag, perfectly dressed in a pink poodle skirt and black-trimmed sweater.

"Are they all in body bags?" asked Ryan.

"This isn't a body bag. This is a collector's protector. These are the rarest of the dolls we're selling and the most controversial and toxic," defended Summer.

"Toxic?" asked Seth.

"Yes. The original Barbie constructed in 1959 had high traces of polyvinyl chloride, better known as PVC. It was used originally to help keep plastics and manmade materials soft. So how cool are these?"

"Summer, did you touch those? I think you are showing signs of being exposed." Seth laughed.

Summer lurched forward and slapped him on the head.

"See? See what I mean — you are turning violent," he yelped.

Summer let out a huge sigh of exasperation.

"Don't you get it? These dolls represent how innocently manufacturers used materials that are now completely toxic and forbidden in toys . . . these Barbies are the perfect metaphor — no, *symbol*, no, *allegory*, no, *image*, I got it, *icon* — for what we are trying to do — raise money for needy neighbors and replace all those toxic jungle gyms!"

"So you are going to sell some toxic Barbies to make a point?"

"It's not like drinking Comet! The whole point is the slow overall exposure and the increased levels that children can acquire with time. You don't die all at once but eventually there is a harmful buildup." Summer crossed her arms over her chest. "Get it?"

Ryan smiled. "Impressive."

"*Cohen!?*" Summer asked.

"How did you exactly find out about these specific dolls?"

"Well, we got this old, old box and it was so obvious it had been in extreme conditions like a basement or attic, just like if you were outside. The more extreme conditions you expose these chemicals to, the more active they become."

"So why don't you just build domes over all the playgrounds and make them air-conditioned with climate control?"

"*Not* funny. Where's the coffee?"

Seth was watching the clock by the time his parents joined them. He needed to be at the mall about an hour before opening to apply the glue for his beard and arrange all the stuffing so it looked real.

"I better roll," said Seth.

"Why? What exactly have you been doing with your volunteer time?"

"Hmmm? Well, I've found a niche market that needed me." He smiled.

"And that is?" interrogated Summer.

"I will tell you all about it at tomorrow's lighting. Actually, I'll just bring a picture." Seth winked and dashed out the door with his skateboard before anyone could ask him details.

When Seth arrived at the mall, he slipped through the empty parking lot and into the back employee doors. He loved this part of the job. He enjoyed being part of the people who were allowed on premises before the mall opened and he loved these quiet times with Clarisse. As he began to strap on his pillows he saw a large shadow in the locker room.

"You're pretty skinny for a Santa," said Buckeye.

Although Seth was surprised, he felt defensive for Clarisse and how she had been hurt.

"Well, you were too drunk for a Santa."

"Hey, kid. You're probably too young to know how hard life can be."

"You're right, but I also know that it makes a difference to those of us who are younger to look up to people who have had it hard." Seth surprised himself with this. It was unusual for him to complete strong sentences without interrupting himself six times to change the focus.

"I get it, kid. I came to wish you luck tonight." Buckeye held out his hand.

"Thanks. I'm going to need it. Those kids are expecting you. The real legacy of Santa is hard to keep up with just a few pillows and fluff." Seth and Buckeye locked eyes.

"The real legacy of Santa is impossible to keep up. Don't try. You'll only hurt someone and they'll never forgive you." Buckeye sat down on the bench and his shoulders slumped as he hung his head.

"What about all the kids you gave hope to? It seems to me you only lost one," said Seth. "Well, make that two."

"What do you mean two? There was only the little boy. That little boy was right. I failed, I lied, and I was a poseur, not someone who could really help. I didn't have money or power or a seat on the chairman's board of any committee. I was just this old actor who looked like Santa, making false promises."

"There is one person who still believes in you."

"Yeah? Who?" asked Buckeye.

"Clarisse," said Seth.

Buckeye hung his head again.

"I guess you're right," he said, looking Seth in the eye.

"About what?"

"I've failed two."

"It's not too late. I know they still need extra help at Santa's Workshop." Seth smiled, hoping to lure him back for the kids tonight. "And it *is* a special night."

Buckeye stood up and turned away. "Sorry, kid. I just can't face it anymore."

Seth felt defeated. He was also slumped over on the bench when he heard Clarisse knock.

"Hey, jolly Old Saint Nick, you don't look so jolly," she said.

"I don't feel so jolly."

"What's up? Trouble at home?"

She was so earnest and sweet, thought Seth.

"No, no. I saw Buckeye and I couldn't convince him to come back. I think I even made matters worse."

"I knew he wouldn't be able to stay away. Somewhere in his heart he wants to watch those kids open their toys and lose themselves in the magic of the night, forgetting everything that is sour about their lives."

"Well, I thought I could get him to take the suit back but he just turned his back and wished me luck," said Seth.

"And you are going to need it. The day before Christmas Eve is a shopping nightmare." Clarisse smiled. "I think you can handle it. Besides, tonight is so much fun, the day will slip away."

Clarisse was right. By the time they opened the gates at Santa's Workshop and the fake glitter snow began to blow there was already a line of about fifty kids.

"What the heck?" said Seth out loud.

Clarisse flashed him a big smile, grabbed a bunch of lollipops out of her pouch, and said: "School's out, silly!"

They were so busy Seth didn't even notice when the sun filled the glass dome and then settled on the other side of the sky. It was night and he barely remembered stopping his jolly laugh for a moment. Just as he was growing tired and felt in desperate need of a super grande coffee he saw his mother and Summer strolling through the mall. At first he thought he was delusional. It had been a long time since he'd had a break and the sweat was pouring down his back under the hot suit. Sure enough, they were headed right toward Santa's Workshop. He tried not to panic.

Seth knew hundreds of people came to the mall to see the workshop, not to sit on Santa's lap. It was a grand display of decorating art and stage set. Every year was a different theme. He slipped down under his beard and consoled himself with the idea that it was impossible for anyone to recognize him.

He was trying to pay attention to the kid on his lap but he couldn't because he saw his father and Marissa join Summer and Kirsten. It could *not* be happening. After this whole week of remaining stealthy and silent about his job he was about to be exposed. He regretted not telling Clarisse that he had money and lived in a big house. He was sure she would hate him. He wanted to tell her but there never seemed to be a right time. She saw him as just another normal kid and he wanted to keep it that way. The moment anyone found out you were from the OC it was clear that life was easier for you. He wished people knew the difference between how good a big car and cool clothes could look and how painful teenage life could be with a broken heart — being ignored or made fun of in school.

And he hadn't wanted to tell his family and friends what he was doing because . . . well, he wasn't sure why. Okay, when he started, it was because of his run-in with mall security. Then there was Clarisse. No way Summer would understand that! Then he'd been afraid that they'd laugh at him — even though he knew they never would. Being Santa had given Seth a chance to be someone other than himself, and he was afraid that if he told people what he was doing, he couldn't be that other person — Santa — anymore. He'd end up being his own slightly geeky self again.

Seth watched as Marissa smiled and held up a really silly pair of red Converse sneakers. Sandy put his arm around her shoulder and Marissa pretended to shoot a basket. Summer and Kirsten rolled their eyes and laughed. The four started to walk in another direction. Seth felt a sigh of relief and smiled into the camera with the kid who had just asked for snow in California.

The impossible dreams, Seth thought. He was sorry he couldn't do anything else for Clarisse but give her some money. It seemed like such a bad consolation prize for losing her faith in Buckeye. As the flash from the camera pulsed in his eyes, Seth waited for the next child. When he hoisted the small girl onto his lap he saw the shadow of Ryan Atwood coming down another corridor. Ryan pulled out his cell phone and talked into it for a moment. Seth glanced around to see Sandy waving to him. Sandy motioned for Ryan to meet them in front of Santa's Workshop.

Seth began to hyperventilate as they all

got closer. He wiped the sweat from his eyes and tried to get Clarisse's attention. He thought if she could shut down Santa's wish-list line he might have a chance of avoiding his family and sneaking away. Clarisse was not paying attention to Seth or any of the children pushing and stepping on one another's toes. She was fixated on Ryan. Seth knew Ryan had what it took when it came to girls, and that his bad-boy-pout lips were attractive to everyone, but he was jealous of the way Clarisse stared so blatantly at him. Just then Clarisse shut down the line. She snapped closed the gate and put up the SANTA NEEDS A NAP sign so fast that Seth thought she had read his mind. She leaped over the candy cane hurdles and grabbed Seth by the arm. Kids and parents moaned and groaned but she just shoved and pushed until she had both herself and Seth free from the stage. Seth was confused, though. They always exited behind the red velvet throne and Clarisse was sprinting toward Seth's family.

"That's him!" she said, breathless. "I would know those eyes anywhere."

"Which one?" asked Seth. He looked at all the bodies swarming through the mall.

Clarisse pointed directly at Ryan and said, "The one in the black T-shirt."

"No. No way. I mean, how can you be sure?" he asked.

Clarisse frowned and her eyes filled with tears. "How can you doubt me? I have waited years for this moment! I know it's him. His name is Ryan."

"How do you know that?" asked Seth.

"Buckeye used to mumble it all the time when he got drunk."

Seth looked up at Ryan. Ryan was obviously uncomfortable. Although he did his best job to hide it, Seth had come to know Ryan's physical reactions to a situation. Seth had spent some time figuring out how

Ryan communicated without ever opening his mouth. It was definitely clear Ryan was uncomfortable. Ryan kept turning his head away from Santa's Workshop and trying to get the family to move in another direction. He ran his fingers through his hair seven times in a matter of seconds. Seth thought about the morning they had been in the pool house together and Ryan had begun to tell Seth a story he never finished. Seth took a deep breath and closed his eyes.

Clarisse dropped Seth's hand. "I'm going to talk to him," she said, almost tripping over her elfin shoes.

"Come on, I'll introduce you," said Seth.

"What? You know him?"

"I live with him, or I guess you can say he lives with me."

"What are you talking about?" She was on the verge of hysteria.

He tried to calm her down by placing his hands on both her shoulders. She pushed him away and pointed a finger in his face. "You tell me what you know about him right now."

"I know that he had a rough life and there is the possibility that his mother spent Christmas in jail but he never told me and I'm almost like his brother."

"Well, we're going to find out." Clarisse spun on her heel and jerked Seth's arm so hard that he almost fell over.

Sandy smiled as Santa and a pretty elfin girl approached.

"Hey, look, maybe we can get a picture with them," said Sandy.

Summer whined, "No, I totally want to get my picture taken on the velvet throne."

Clarisse was right in front of Ryan. Ryan looked down at the floor.

"Have you ever been here before?" Clarisse almost yelled at him.

Marissa looked at Ryan. "Do you know her?"

"No," Ryan replied quickly.

Seth was sure he was going to pass out if he didn't pull off his beard.

Sandy stepped between Ryan and Clarisse. "Young lady, can I help you?"

"I just want to know if his mother ever went to jail at Christmas?" Clarisse asked with tears in her own eyes.

Kirsten took a step toward Ryan. Ryan would not look up.

Sandy turned to Clarisse. "Young lady, that is a very personal question to ask someone you do not know."

"Oh, I know him," she snapped.

"Ryan? We need some explanation here," said Sandy.

Ryan shrugged. He didn't seam reluctant to speak. . . . more like he was unable to.

"Your name is Ryan. When you were six

years old your mother went to jail and you were so angry you came back here and accused Santa of failing you."

The shock on everyone's face was so intense the entire mall seemed to be moving in slow motion.

Clarisse continued, "I've waited ten years to see you walk through those doors again. This is a miracle and I can only thank Seth that you came to see him."

Summer looked at Marissa. "Seth?"

Kirsten shook her head, "I'm sorry, young lady, but we don't even know where Seth is right now."

Clarisse poked the red-faced Santa in the belly.

"Didn't you come to see him?" Clarisse asked, pointing at Santa.

Sandy laughed. "Santa? Well, we did want our picture taken but I don't know what that has to do with our son."

Seth pulled at the edges of his white beard, showing his face for a moment.

Ryan looked up at Seth and could not contain himself. Ryan began to laugh, then Marissa and Summer began to laugh, and soon everyone had fallen over into a hysterical fit of giggles.

Clarisse was confounded and certainly confused.

"I didn't tell them what I was doing," said Seth.

"They didn't know you were volunteering?"

"Oh my god, Seth, that is so cute. You were volunteering as Santa?" Summer ran to him and gave him a very big kiss on the lips.

Seth was embarrassed and pulled away.

Clarisse smiled. "You must be Seth's girlfriend. He told me a lot about you," she said.

"Oh. Well, right now I guess we're, well, whatever, but it is totally sweet that he was playing Santa. How could I resist him that way?" she said, punching him lightly in his pillow fluff.

Clarisse took a deep breath and said, "Yeah, how could you resist him?" She smiled at Seth.

Sandy had regained composure and placed a hand on Ryan's back.

"Ryan? Why didn't you tell us?"

"What was to tell? It was just another horrible memory and my life has changed so much since then. I don't like to think about it," said Ryan. "It just ruins Christmas the more I dwell on it."

Sandy Cohen put his arm around Ryan's shoulders and gave him a tight embrace.

"I'm sorry. I know you want to forget . . . but there's one person who hasn't forgotten, and it's ruined his Christmas," said Clarisse. "Do you think you could tell Santa you know it wasn't his fault?"

"Seth?" asked Ryan, confused.

"No. The person who played Santa all these years felt so horrible after your mother went to prison that he started down a very bad path."

Ryan was taken back. "But I was a kid, a lost little kid. How could he take it personally?"

Clarisse shrugged. "You know how it is. There are some things we never forget."

Ryan sighed. "No matter how hard we try."

"I know he's here somewhere. He never misses tonight. This is the night all the orphans and foster kids come for the party. Even if he isn't working he'll hide in one of our favorite places to see the kids open their presents. Will you come with me and look for him?"

"What about Santa's Workshop?" asked Seth.

Clarisse pulled off her green velvet hat and bolero jacket and handed them to Summer.

"Tell the kids no pushing, no shoving, and only give them a lollipop as a last resort. We'll be back soon."

Summer smiled and walked toward the velvet ropes where kids and parents gathered with their bags.

"This is cool. I'm like the bouncer!" She smiled. "Come on, Cohen!"

Clarisse helped Seth on with his beard and readjusted his pillows to make him look jolly. She looked deep into his eyes and smiled. "Thanks for the miracle. I believe in you." She kissed him softly on the nose and waved one last time before she and Ryan disappeared into the crowded mall.

10

The sun began to set on the edge of the Cohens' pool. Ryan looked at himself in the mirror and smiled. He was dressed in a new tuxedo and his hair was slightly slicked back — he looked sharp. Although there had been a pact that no one would give gifts this year, Sandy had made sure that both boys found Tom Ford tuxedos in their closets with all the right accessories to attend Newport's gala event on Christmas Eve. New Playgrounds for Needy Neighbors wasn't just a local event; so many radio stations and newspapers were now involved that Kirsten had to find a larger hall and make room for double the original guest list. They were expecting large amounts of media from all over southern and northern California and several high-profile politicians and movie stars had requested the clearance to stop by even if they did not remain for the entire event.

Ryan pulled awkwardly at the bow tie and wondered if he really had to wear it. He stuffed it into his pocket and joined the others in the main house.

Marissa looked beautiful. She was wearing a full-length silver gown that made her look like an angel on top of the tree. She smiled as Ryan entered, and waved with enthusiasm. It had been so long since Ryan had seen Marissa so happy. She glowed.

Julie Cooper winked at Ryan. He had sworn to keep all her secrets and as she sat perched on the edge of the Cohens' couch in her jeweled red dress it was hard to imagine that she was the same woman he had watched saw a few inches off a coffee table so it would fit perfectly under a window in a crowded apartment.

Summer paced. It was true that Kirsten was in charge of the event but it had begun to feel like her own. She had never felt so invested in anything since the comic book fiasco. She hoped that they reached their goal by selling all of the Barbies that had been refurbished by her very cracked, dry, paint-stained hands. It was clear the moment Summer was done being humble she was going back to Bliss Spa for a par-affin wax treatment on her hands.

Kirsten came down the stairs and smiled at Summer. They had purchased matching dresses in different colors that had been redyed to make the perfect Barbie pink and Barbie blue chiffon. Kirsten placed her hand on Summer's shoulder and gave her a kiss on the forehead.

Jimmy Cooper stood next to Sandy Cohen, discussing the chance of creating a coalition that could legally restrict areas in South America for endangered species while still allowing divers and recreational enthusiasts to play among them.

As Seth looked around the room he felt a harmony. He knew Buckeye was spending tonight making up for lost time. The lines to see Santa on Christmas Eve were rumored to snake through the entire mall and although Seth missed Clarisse he was happy not to be suffocating under the mass of pillows.

"Okay," said Seth. "Gather around and let's go through the significance of the past eight days before we head off to the most awaited event of the year."

Summer and Kirsten bowed their heads.

"As many of you know, this special holiday was created by myself to incorporate the traditions of Christmas and Hanukkah.

Chrismukkah is the best time of the year and I am grateful you all made an extraordinary effort to participate. There were many surprises but that is the nature of miracles. Tonight we light the candles of the menorah and the Christmas tree lights to signify all the great gifts we have learned."

Sandy smiled and patted Jimmy on the back. "I've learned that although sons are great, it is a lot of fun to have a daughter to help you in the office, and daughters are definitely more organized! A toast to Marissa for breaking through the box barrier between my door and desk and helping me find a new way to make room for art on the boardwalk."

Marissa blushed. Sandy continued: "I'd like to nominate Marissa for learning the most about herself, for changing the view of the board, and for creating new venues for artists on the beach."

Everyone clapped enthusiastically but

Kirsten interrupted. "No, Marissa. I know how hard you worked and I do not deny you a moment of your accomplishment. But I would like to nominate Summer as having learned the most about her natural talents as a woman in business, an incredible marketing strategist, and a reckoning force of unlimited energy in making sure we get dangerous toxins away from children."

Kirsten raised a glass of champagne in Summer's direction and clapped loudly.

Julie Cooper cleared her throat. "Actually, I would like to nominate Ryan Atwood for his ability to wield a hammer, nail, spackle, sand, and all of it on quick demand, as well as his kind heart and genuine interest in making homes better for those living without luxury. Ryan, I was very proud to work with you and I'm not sure who learned more." Before Julie's voice could crack, she threw back her champagne and finished her glass.

Jimmy Cooper stood up. "Well, I guess that leaves Seth. The strange part is I told Seth to go out every day and practice random acts of kindness. What I never expected was that he would spend his days sweating through a velvet Santa suit so both rich and poor kids would not be disappointed. I want to nominate Seth for his ability to encourage us all to do what we feared and force us to learn about ourselves."

There was a large round of applause from everyone.

Seth cleared his throat. "I think we have a tie here."

Kirsten placed her hand on Seth's shoulder. "No, we have a very good reason to be proud of ourselves and be thankful for not only the security we have but the love and friendship we can rely on."

"Mom. Don't cry. This will turn out to be a total chicktastrophe if all your makeup starts running before the auction!"

As the group prepared to leave for the gala ball and they gathered up the last of the purses and car keys, Ryan went into the kitchen to turn out the pool lights. He looked across the glittering sky and high above the sliver of the moon he swore he saw the silhouette of a sleigh. He laughed at himself for never giving up the dream that one day Santa would come to his house. He realized that the greatest gift he had been given during the eight days of Chrismukkah was the chance to for-give — and hopefully *forget* the *past*.